EVE'S HOUR
by
Norma Newcomb

Author of "THE QUESTING HEART,"
"A SINGING HEART," *etc.*

When Eve Barkwell decided to accept Lois Hill's challenge to battle, in which the first skirmish was to be a "scrappy-cat" race on the waters of Maryland's Eastern Shore, the citizens of Sather called her a foolish girl who had a tiger by the tail. For Eve was an easygoing watchmaker in her father's jewelry store, while Lois' father owned a national drug firm and the Hills were the first summer family of Sather.

Yet Eve had certain advantages: a reputation for honest work, a reputation for being the first to give anyone a helping hand in an emergency, a reputation for courage and kindness.

Therefore the all-out war, of which the sailing contest was only a symbol and a precursor, promised to be dramatic and prolonged, with very high stakes.

EVE'S HOUR

EVE'S HOUR

by

NORMA NEWCOMB

By
Sharon Publications, Inc.
Closter, NJ

Copyright © MCMLXIII by Arcadia House
Published by
Sharon Publications Inc.
Closter, N.J. 07624
Printed in the U.S.A.
Cover illustrations by Simon Galkin
ISBN 0-89531-127-5

EVE'S HOUR

Chapter 1

Eve resolved at breakfast that she wouldn't lose her temper, come what may. At seven-forty-five, however, she almost did. Rod's telephone voice was so rude. "Kid," it said, "find yourself another sucker. Boy, I wouldn't even drive you to the morgue."

He waited, presumably for pleas or apologies or both. Having counted to ten, Eve counted to twenty. The silly device worked. To her delight, she was able to say pleasantly, "Well, I'll miss our rides, of course, but never you mind about that."

Eve broke the connection before he could. She checked the stove, the lights in all the rooms. On the service porch of her cottage, she got into raincoat and rain boots and picked out the largest umbrella in the stand. The umbrella was useless, though, after she'd reached the river road. The strong wind almost tore it from her grasp. Blown this way and that, the umbrella kept only a trickle of rain from her at best and had the general effect of slowing her gait exasperatingly. Eve finally closed the thing, reasoning she could dry her face after she reached her shop.

Oddly, the storm pleased her. She loved the storm sounds, the hard-running river, the frenzies of the maples and horse chestnuts. Most of all, she loved the iron-gray lid the storm seemed to have clamped over the sky. Hemmed in by the gray, Sather had the charming appearance of a snug little storybook village, capable of withstanding any assault the elements could loose. A childish illusion, of course, yet so satisfying to the eye and spirit that Eve had to halt when she reached the bridge to see her fill.

A truck came rumbling through the storm. Eve recognized the motor and kept her back turned to the bridge entrance, hoping that Rod would drive on. He did, but only for about fifteen feet. The brakes squeaked. Presently the truck backed up. Rod rolled the cab window down and yelled: "Okay, Eve, hop in, darn it."

Instead, Eve mounted the bridge and ambled over it to the foot of Morris Street. A comical thing happened. Rod kept inching the truck along beside her, yelling for her not to be silly, yelling for her not to be stubborn, yelling for her not to make him angry. Eve smiled at him from time to time, but when she reached Moe's Diner she nipped inside.

Immense in wrinkled white, Moe stared. Like a father with his chick, he waddled to her and helped her with her rain hat and raincoat. He made her take the table nearest the radiator. He got a carafe and filled it with coffee, and then he got the biggest cup he could find and served her. Throughout, he scolded her. "You nuts? Days like this you call Moe if you're stuck. Ain't anybody told you about pneumonia or anything? Kids like you should have their noggins examined."

Eve asked bitterly: "Do you hate me or love

me, Moe? A girl can take it either way. I just want to know."

"Huh?"

"Oh, I'm the villain, all right. See the girl who said no! Dreadful of me, really. After all, Moe, what's land? Why cling to a mere five acres when others want them for recreational purposes? Where's the old town spirit?"

Moe asked casually, "You want me to bust him on the nose?"

Eve swiveled about to look. Yup, there was Rod getting out of his truck to give her a bad time.

Stiff-legged and red-faced, he came to the door and wrenched it open as if he wanted to tear it from its hinges. Once inside, with powerful Moe taking his measure, Rod calmed down somewhat, but there remained in his watery gray eyes a fire that Eve didn't like. When Rod asked if he could join her, Eve told him no.

He joined her anyway. "Just keep on like that," he warned, "and you won't have a friend in town. Not that you have many right now. Who are you to call us land grabbers? Who are you to call us liars?"

"Will it clear by tomorrow, do you think? I'm to get my boat from Mr. Wiley tomorrow."

Rod jabbed a long forefinger toward her. "You get this straight, Eve. The Town Council offered you a fair price for your land. I saw to that. If you don't sell it, I'll see personally that the Town Council begins that eminent domain stuff to get the land anyway. You're worse than a dog in a manger. You aren't using that land, and you won't use it, and you know it."

Eve grinned, finding it easy to keep her temper with Rod becoming angrier every second. "Moe," she asked, "don't you protect your customers from nuisances like this?"

Moe waved Rod toward the counter stools.

"In other words," Rod asked, "you're playing it tough, Eve?"

"Practical; not tough," Eve corrected him. "I expect to marry some year, have children. The land is for my children."

"We offer a thousand an acre!"

"For lovely land spread along Town Creek?

You're certainly generous! In five years that land will be worth ten thousand an acre. Add improvements, a small-boat harbor and marina, say, and it will be worth fifty thousand an acre."

Rod couldn't have looked more stunned had she clubbed him.

Eve said coolly: "I'll take fifteen thousand an acre, Rod. That's my price. If the Town Council wants to make the deal, fine. Reasonable?"

He said with feeling: "Boy, are you nuts! Boy, do we have to educate you!"

And yet, Eve thought after he'd stalked out, she really was being reasonable. Actually, if the town used her acres for recreational purposes, the local tourist business would boom. Folks would flock to Sather from all along the seaboard to enjoy the sailing, the swimming, the fishing, the hiking, the riding. Existing stores and shops would thrive. New stores and shops would be built. More and more money would be spent in town, so more and more jobs would be created for the townspeople. Considering all the benefits the town would derive from the land, her asking price was definitely reasonable.

Moe said: "You can't win, youngster. I ain't saying you should give the land away, but I am saying you better not hold out for the last penny. You know why? Because you're in business, just like me. Okay. So to keep local business, you have to play ball. If you don't play ball, they take their business elsewhere. See what I mean?"

"No one cuts off his nose to spite his face, Moe. No sane person, anyway. I get the local watch-repairing business because I know my trade. Sure, there are a dozen watchmakers within twenty miles, and the trade could go to them. But the watches I repair keep time, and everyone knows that."

"Just the same—"

"Moe, I went into hock for that land because I do want to build there some day. Two years ago, when I paid five hundred an acre, Rod was one of the persons who claimed I'd been clipped. Sather could have bought that land then. But the Town Council didn't see its value then, and I doubt the Council would see it now if Mr. Hill hadn't pointed it out to them."

"If you think you can battle the Council *and* Mr. Hill, you're nuts."

"Just a helpless girl trying to get along, Moe. I certainly won't start any battle, I guarantee that."

It was still raining violently when Eve returned to Morris Street. Not expecting anyone to offer a ride, she bent into the wind and rain and pushed along doggedly for three blocks. That effort brought her to the pink frame one-story building that housed the *Sather Record,* and as good luck would have it, Miss Elias happened to be facing the street windows when Eve paused to catch her breath under the aluminum awning. Miss Elias at once invited her indoors to warm her bones and give her side of the story for publication. "You may as well be told," Miss Elias said crisply, "that you offended many persons at the Town Council meeting last evening. Some claimed you are insufferably arrogant. Others claimed you are insufferably selfish. Almost everyone agreed that you lack proper community spirit. Do you wish such thinking to become widespread? Of course not!

So, my dear, you will talk for publication. I advise it. My advice is always worth following."

"Print what you think best, ma'am. I'm merely a watchmaker. How in the world would I know what to say or how to say it? Off the record, I was never told that my land is wanted for recreational purposes. Supervisor Wilcox sprang it on me cold, before everyone. The ridiculous price he offered was offered almost as a bone is to a hungry dog. Well, the complete lack of courtesy made me angry. Probably I did seem arrogant in my anger. Probably I did say more than I should have said. On the other hand, why should I allow anyone to bully me into parting with that land? There's other land. Perhaps my location is best for their purposes, but still—"

"It is." Miss Elias knit her brows and gazed thoughtfully out at the rain. "Actually," she conceded, "Mr. Wilcox's tactics were all wrong. I think that was because he assumed you'd not part with the land regardless of what price was offered. Still, he should have approached you privately. I told him so after the meeting."

"May I ask a question, Miss Elias?"

"Certainly."

"What do they really want my land for? I didn't sleep much last night. I was too upset. After all, this is my home town, and I've known most of the folks in town all my life. It isn't pleasant, believe me, to have all your friends boo you as they booed me last night. Anyway, I couldn't sleep. So I thought about the recreational setup Supervisor Wilcox mentioned. And it suddenly occurred to me, ma'am, that the whole thing is preposterous. Wiley's Anchorage farther up Town Creek, for instance, can accommodate three times the boats that are moored there each summer. Right behind the Anchorage are at least twenty wooded acres which would be ideal for park, recreational and other purposes. You see?"

"Mr. Hill owns them, though."

"And about a thousand acres more, ma'am. He'd not miss five or ten or even all twenty of those acres."

"Unfortunately, Eve, his house stands quite close to those acres. He would hardly want hordes of tourists racketing about near his house, now would he?"

Meeting her black eyes squarely, Eve said: "I think the Town Council is trying to develop a light-industry area along Town Creek, ma'am. That's the only answer that makes sense to me."

"It's my understanding that they want the land for the purpose that was stated last evening, Eve. I've already written a story concerning that. I might as well add that I'm planning to write an editorial in favor of the development. My dear girl, what is Sather most of the year? Simply another sleepy town on the Eastern Shore of Maryland. Very well. Then, clearly, the town must do something to attract so many tourists and vacationists that our people will have ample money to live on during the dull months of the year. And consider the effect upon your own business. How much do you take in a month, on an average, between November and last March?"

"About a thousand a month."

"Gross income, of course. I was referring to net income."

Eve wondered if the woman could be trusted. She decided the gamble was worth taking. "I was referring to net income, too," she said simply.

Miss Elias blinked. "My dear girl, that's impossible!"

"Not really, ma'am. What you've forgotten is that my father began my training when I was ten. I'm now twenty-three. Well, if you have a good teacher and thirteen years of experience and a natural aptitude for a trade, you become rather proficient. The Bennett Jewelers in Philadelphia think so, at any rate. They offered to make me supervisor of their watch-repairing department. Naturally, I refused. So they made me a counter offer. I handle their difficult clocks and chronometers and repeaters—chime watches, that is. My minimum fee is twenty dollars."

Miss Elias asked indignantly: "Are you trying to mislead me, young lady?"

Eve chuckled, amused by the flashing black eyes. "You can always check up, ma'am, can't you?"

"You mean to sit there and say that if the

whole town boycotted your shop, you'd still earn a good living right here in town?"

"Yes."

Miss Elias wagged her head, her vaunted composure obviously shaken for a change. She finally said testily: "That does make a difference, you know. There was much talk last evening of teaching you a badly needed lesson. Directly after you left, Rod proposed a boycott of the Clepsydra. Fortunately, wiser heads prevailed. Do you plan to marry Ken Elston?"

Eve said: "Whoa!"

Miss Elias chuckled. "You'd be astonished, dear, how often that technique works. Nine times out of ten people make honest answers to suddenly popped questions. But I certainly wasn't trying to trap you. It was Ken Elston who got the boycott proposal tabled. Rod yelled that Ken was protecting you because Ken thought you would marry him. Quite an argument after that, believe me."

Eve drew a deep breath. She decided that if Miss Elias had gotten useful information from their talk, so had she. She also decided that loyal Ken Elston would have to be given a grand home-cooked dinner. Imagine Ken siding against Supervisor Wilcox and his very own father!

Chapter 2

The Clepsydra was an attractive shop possessed of two large show windows that jutted forward on each side of the gold and crimson entrance door. Billy Taylor was already working at the bench in the right-hand window when a wind-blown and rather sodden Eve reached the pseudo-log building. Billy gave her a happy grin. "Real blaster, Miss Eve, huh? Golly, is that river running wild! You know what Mr. Peabody told me? He said if the rain don't let up, lots of his land will be flooded."

"It usually is this time of year. But there's never erosion there to speak of. After the river nicely irrigates that land, Mr. Peabody seeds it with annuals and ends up winning all the prizes the Sather Garden Club offers."

"Not this year," Billy vowed. "I read in a book that a real smart character can take seedling dwarf rhododendrons and stick them in pots, little pots, and make miniatures out of them. One prize he won't win is the potted-plant prize. I'm gonna sweep the board."

"Without blooms? I doubt it."

Billy chuckled. "You get 'em blooming in September and October, Miss Eve, if you know what you're doing. Only don't tell him, huh?"

Eve noticed she was dripping rain onto the new, gold-flecked tangerine linoleum tile. She went through the shop and her office and the storeroom to the rear door. She arranged her rain gear to drip-dry on the small enclosed porch, then changed into uniform and work shoes in her office. She decided that her first duty was to Ken Elston. She telephoned him at the bank, but the receptionist-telephone operator there connected her with Senior, not Junior. Senior was professionally jovial only until he recognized Eve's voice. Predictably, a growl then came into his voice. "Young lady," he growled, "I'd like to paddle you. What sort of behavior was that last night? I don't say any-one should love everyone, but I do say that an intelligent businesswoman ought at least to pre-tend to like everyone."

"You'll be happy to know, I hope, that I've resolved never to lose my temper again, come what may."

"The horse is out of the barn."

"At the next meeting, I'll apologize to Super-visor Wilcox."

The statement evidently astonished him. "Well, now," he rumbled, "that's better, much better. You'll find it pays, Eve, to treat others as you expect them to treat you. Now, then, what can I do for you?"

"Actually, sir, I was calling your son."

"Oh?"

Eve said bluntly: "I wanted to invite him to dinner at my cottage this Friday evening."

"Oh?"

Eve couldn't resist joshing him. "Oh, it happens, sir. A fellow is handsome or personable or a good talker, and the first thing you know, girls beat a path to his door."

He harumphed and sputtered, obviously wiggling on a hook not to his liking. If he disapproved of his son's interest in a person in trade, he could hardly disapprove of her comfortable income. Further, she did own those five acres along Town Creek, land he darned well knew would be worth a small fortune some day.

He funked the issue. "Ken is out on business," he finally growled. "I'll leave your message on his desk."

Knowing he'd do no such thing, Eve thanked him politely and hung up and jotted down a reminder on her calendar pad to telephone Ken that afternoon.

Billy had a technical problem waiting for her when she went up front to tackle her first watch of the day. Looking utterly frustrated, Billy pointed at the Elgin lady's baguette in his movement holder and said: "It keeps stopping, Miss Eve. It runs for maybe two or three minutes, then conks out."

"Is it in beat?"

The boy, all of seventeen and startlingly hand-some, chose to be offended. His violet eyes flashed. His left hand went up to ruffle his golden hair agitatedly. Had his crutches been within easy reach and the day fair, he'd probably have stalked out to brood over a glass of milk down the street.

"Miss Eve," he said aggrievedly, "don't you think I've got eyes? Can't I put the loupe in my eye and see to it that the roller jewel is centered between the banking pins? You think I can't learn to do a little thing like that, Miss Eve? If I can't do a little thing like that, how come some of the watches I repair run pretty good?"

"Mr. William Taylor, I apologize!"

He was genuinely dumbfounded. Next, he became worried. "Hey," he asked worriedly, "you sick, Miss Eve?"

"Glory," Eve said, "am I glad I'm not *your* girl! Stop being such a shifty character! Stop trying to put me on the defensive! My question was reasonable, and certainly no insult was intended."

She dragged a stool over to his bench and examined the Elgin movement. She got the balance wheel going with a flick of utility tweezers. It was at once obvious that the problem involved the escapement. That discovery brought her face to face with the necessity to make a rather delicate decision. To let him or not let him adjust the left pallet jewel? If she did let him and he goofed, she might have to buy a new pallet. Yet if she didn't let him try, how would he ever learn to handle such problems without help?

"How are your nerves today?" she asked. "Did you or didn't you whup Sally Peabody at chess last evening?"

"Three games," he chortled. "Did she stew! And she got madder and madder just because I said chess was for men, not girls!"

For better or worse, Eve made the decision. "The answer to this problem, young fellow, is in the pallet jewels. So get out your manual and study the section on pallet-jewel adjustment. Then when you think you know what ought to be done, go ahead and do it. If you wreck the pallet, though, I'll nail you by the ears to the entrance door."

It happened to the poor fellow as it had once happened to her. He went pale with nervousness, self-doubt, fear. He said huskily: "Gee, Miss Eve, maybe I ought to practise on a big watch first. This pallet is so darned tiny!"

Eve just went to her own bench and laid out her tools for the day's work.

"Miss Eve?" Billy begged.

"If I were seventeen, and handicapped, and had no family and little money, Billy, I'd welcome every opportunity to learn what I was given. I'd become a master watchmaker. Why? Because some day I would want to open a shop such as this and earn a good living for myself and my family. The pallet won't shoot you, you know."

An interesting thought occurred to Billy Taylor. "Hey, Miss Eve, do you think Sally would marry me once I was a master watchmaker?"

"Only Sally can tell you that."

"You know what Sally said?"

"Will you work, please?"

"She said," Billy told her dreamily, "that I'm lots of fun for a crippled guy."

A lump came into Eve's throat. This boy, she decided, would have to be supervised. Not by a dimwit girl of twenty-three, either, a girl who couldn't keep her own emotional house in order. What he needed urgently, hang it, was the counsel of an older woman, for only older women possessed the broad knowledge, the patience, the tact and the good will to nudge him along the road he had to take.

She now *ordered* Billy to work. Her crisp voice was effective. Onto Billy's face came a do-or-die expression, and then, at last, the shop was so quiet you could hear the eternal whispering of the clocks and watches along the walls and in the display counters. Contentedly, Eve went to work, too, cleaning a sixteen-size Waltham pocket watch to get her eyes and hands in the old work groove.

It was a productive morning for her. The ever-thickening rain practically washed all traffic from Morris Street, and not a pedestrian came through their block. Because no one bothered her, not even Billy, Eve was able to clean not only the pocket watch but three wrist watches as well. Then, nicely warmed up, she was able to do three balance-staff jobs in addition before lunch.

Her production dazzled Billy. Bogged down in his escapement problem, he looked wistfully at the completed jobs on her bench rack. "How'd you get so fast?" he wanted to know. "Even when I have no trouble, Miss Eve, I can't do three cleanings in a day."

"Practise. Eternal repetition. And please don't worry about speed! It comes through the years. That's the only way it comes, gradually. If you try to force it, you end up producing a lot of watches that don't keep time."

Billy studied the pallet in the pallet holder. "You want to look at this pallet, Miss Eve? I've had it over the alcohol flame so much it's blue-black."

Eve gamely said no. Then, to make certain she'd not weaken to protect her bankroll, she headed for Holloway's Drugstore for lunch.

It was a blunder.

Lois Hill was there, almost inevitably, and the daughter of the great Jared Hill was in the ideal mood for a scrap. Lois said loudly and quite cheerfully: "My, Eve, I never expected you to show your face today! Let me call Rod! Rod wants to shoot you, I think."

All eyes swung to them. Eve hesitated, then went matter-of-factly to Lois' table and sat down. "Rod shot and missed," she said laconically. "Do you recommend the roast beef today?"

"Poison."

The girl's deep gray eyes danced.

"Is that a description of the roast beef or a recommendation, Lois?"

"Miss Hill, please."

Dorothy Holloway came to their table for Eve's order. Dorothy was grand. Dorothy said with considerable warmth: "Always nice to see you, Eve. How your lovely face brightens a dull day!"

Could Lois take a hint?

Sure she could!

All of nineteen, much too intense, cat-quick

mentally, Lois said: "Ah, why brawl? Let there be peace, sweet peace, in Sather. Have you seen my new boat? Daddy had it made in Maine for me. Mission: to whup you soundly on Race Day, Eve."

Dorothy teased: "That will be the day, Miss Hill. Why, Eve beat you by a mile last year and two miles the year before."

"Well, isn't that proof I'm improving?"

She was an odd girl, Eve thought. When she laughed at herself, as she was doing now, she was downright lovable. But it was so seldom she laughed at herself! Usually she took herself, her family's name, her family's position so seriously she was downright intolerable.

"Furthermore," Lois informed them, "I spent the winter in Florida, taking sailing lessons. I found out what I've been doing incorrectly, too. Girls, it pleases me to report I can now tack a sailboat so close to the wind it's fantastic."

Eve doubted that. Tacking a boat required talent. You might learn to do a fair job, but you never did an expert job unless you had sailing in your blood. She congratulated Lois, however, and politely said she was looking forward to a good race next month.

Lois spoiled it all, though, by saying flatly: "Oh, it'll be a good race, all right. The Hills have two interesting summer projects, pet. I'm to whup you on Race Day, and Daddy is to whup you on that land question. Charming?"

Eve almost lost her temper, because at that point everyone except Dorothy Holloway cheered.

Chapter 3

Jared Algernon Hill was displeased. A thin, graying, rather cold-faced man, he announced his displeasure during a stroll with his daughter about his summer estate. "It displeases me," he stated, "that you babble, Lois. One might expect that of other young women, but not of you. You know better, or should know better."

A fetching sight that warm, sunlit April morning, Lois pointed a forefinger at herself and screeched: "Stupid!"

Mr. Hill was not amused. "The watchful person, the silent person, is the person who succeeds in life. It is a foolish person who puts an Eve Barkwell on guard, so to speak."

"Blah."

"Lois?"

"Daddy?"

"You must never try me too far. I might decide the discipline of work would have a salutary effect upon your over-all development."

A less spirited girl might have met his icy gray eyes and quailed. Lois Hill met them all right, but she didn't quail. "Mother begs me to join her in Paris," Lois announced. "It might be amusing. Shall I join my mother in Paris?"

"Is that a threat, Lois?"

"Were you threatening, Daddy?"

They came to a lovely view of white birch and rolling green lawn and blue river. A scrappy-cat was being sailed upstream with the wind. The big sail was full almost to the bursting point, and the little boat was cleaving along between two great ribbons of spray. Lois didn't need binoculars to determine the identity of the girl in the stern of the boat. Only Eve Barkwell sailed that way, as if she owned the winds and the sea.

"Isn't she lovely?" Lois asked her father. "I

have to say, Daddy, that I've never met a lovelier girl than Eve Barkwell. And I'm not talking about her physical appearance, either. She's stacked as all girls are stacked, and brunettes are just brunettes after all. What I'm talking about is her quality of loveliness. Do you know what she'll be some day?"

"The usual dull housewife, I dare say. The girls in her social group usually become such, I'm afraid."

"No, sir. She may be a housewife, but she'll never be dull. She'll be a lady, you wait and see."

"You're a clairvoyant, then? How interesting."

When they reached the white marble bench, Lois sat down to watch the boat on the river. Now the boat was angling away from Kingfisher's Point, coming about in a great semicircle. It occurred to Lois that Eve Barkwell was doing some training for Race Day. First the two-mile run from Town Creek to Kingfisher's Point; then the run upstream to Plain-dealing Cove; then the last run back to the finish line before the Sather Yacht Club.

The tacking was both beautiful and educational. Not once did the big sail luff. Slippage was kept to a minimum by the deft use of the rudder. Each time the boat threatened to slip wide of the wind, Eve Barkwell pumped the tiller and brought the bow around again to make good yardage.

Lois said realistically: "I'm not good enough to beat her, Daddy. See that trick she's using? Well, I know that trick, too. But you have practically to sense when to use it and when not to use it. If you use it prematurely, you swing across the wind, and you luff, and then the boom comes around and—"

"Why aren't you practising?"

Lois rolled her eyes self-deprecatingly. "No ambition," she explained. "I used to be ambitious. This will jar you, I'm sure, but I used to dream of becoming a teacher. Fie! How dare I think of entering so lowly a profession, I, the daughter of the Hill Ethical Drugs Company! So!"

"Merely a childish notion, Lois, as evidenced by your low grades over the years."

"Oh, and I was booted out of college, too, never forget that. Dear Miss Hill, you appear temperamentally unsuited, blah, blah, blah. But I didn't care, Daddy. If you wish to become something and your father forbids it, why study to be something you can't be?"

The long look she gave him troubled Jared Hill. It was all well and good for him to think he had done his best for her. By George, he had done his best, and he had won for her a security and a luxury few young ladies her age enjoyed. But if she were unhappy, what did all his efforts really amount to? She envied Eve Barkwell! Why? Because Eve Barkwell was lovely, popular? No. Simply because Eve Barkwell worked at what she wanted to work at and lived as she wanted to live.

Jared Hill sat down on the marble bench and trained his binoculars on the dwindling scrappy-cat across the river. An arresting picture leapt to his eye. Now Miss Eve Barkwell was standing on the starboard gunwale of her craft, one foot holding the tiller steady, one hand holding the boom line. How cockily and gracefully she stood; how engaging she looked in her young, healthy girl's way in her yellow shorts and brown T-shirt! Yet though the sight was pleasing, it was also vexing. Frowning, Mr. Hill put the glasses back into the case.

"Would you like a job?" he asked Lois. "I'm sure something interesting could be found in headquarters. I discussed that very thing with David only last week. It will be your company, too, when I'm gone. It might be to your advantage to know something about the business."

"Doug keeps me informed."

"Really? I wonder. David and I rarely discuss policy with Doug. Do you know, for example, that we're contemplating a merger with the Kranick outfit?"

"I didn't even know there was a Kranick outfit."

Mr. Hill relaxed, glad to be on familiar business ground. "Oh, there's one, all right. An interesting organization. They're particularly aggressive sales people. They market their products all over the world, despite the limitations of those products. So it occurred to me about a year ago that if they were to merge with us, there could be developed a strong world-wide organization capable of cornering at least ten percent of the ethical drugs business. I felt Mr. Kranick out in Vienna last year. He was loath to agree he needed us more than we needed him. So, my dear, your clever father whipsawed them between lowered prices abroad and sterner sales competition here at home. Mr. Kranick perceived the wisdom of considering our proposition, and I suspect the merger will be accomplished this autumn."

"Did you visit Mother?"

"Now, now . . ."

"Well, why not?" Lois demanded indignantly. "She is the mother of your children, and she is the woman who married you when you were just a penniless chemist."

"We've been through all that," Jared Hill said wearily. "The fact remains that either I outgrew her or she outgrew me. In any event, continuation of our marriage was quite impossible. There's never any point in opening old wounds."

"You happen to be wrong! I asked Dr. Hale about that just the other day. Surgeons sometimes open old wounds for debridement and other purposes."

Mr. Hill was baffled by the complexities of her intellect and emotions. This was the same girl who could ask him to fire an elevator operator because she disliked the wart on his nose!

"I find you intolerably sentimental," he informed her coldly. "I must also state that I fail to understand you. You come here for the express purpose of defeating Miss Barkwell humiliatingly. You deliberately fan the anger of people who hoped to see her land integrated into a vast recreational complex. Yet you call her lovely, you call her a lady. In short, you both like and admire her. Quite confusing, to say the least."

She gave him the sort of look that frequently baffled him, too—a look that suggested he was quite ignorant on the subject of women, and hopelessly ignorant, at that.

Mr. Hill retreated to safer ground.

"Let's get down to cases," he told her. "It does not suit my purpose to have Miss Barkwell on guard. It was my hope, indeed, that she would consider me her friend. The fact is that our position in this land matter is a delicate one. We have these acres, a thousand of them, and I certainly don't want anyone to propose we give a few of them to Sather. I will not have commotion at my very gates. I hoped to persuade Miss Barkwell that she owed it to her home town to be generous. And I fancy I might have succeeded in that had you not babbled to her. Now you have created complications."

Lois grinned, cheerfully impenitent. "Hurrah for me, Daddy! It would be a dull summer for you, wouldn't it, if you didn't have a complication to keep you busy?"

"This land matter means a great deal to me, Lois. Let me brief you. I expect to retire next year. I have a coronary condition, and Dr. Hale thinks retirement is in order. My thought was to build a small plant right here in Sather, a research and development plant I could keep an eye on without straining myself unduly. That's the thing you've jeopardized, and that's why I'm displeased with you."

Lois stared.

Mr. Hill decided to insure her silence in the future. "It was my thought," he continued, "to bring your Doug Chalmers here as general manager. If you're to marry him, a proper berth must be found for him. I can hardly ease him into the headquarters hierarchy without offending men many years his senior, men the company must promote as vacancies open up."

"On Eve Barkwell's land?"

"Yes."

"But the Town Council wouldn't agree! Why, that's one of the prettiest areas in Sather!"

"Supervisor Wilcox is in my vest pocket, so to speak."

Lois whistled. "Does Doug know?" she asked excitedly. "Daddy, is he coming down this summer?"

"I never divulge my plans until I have some assurance they're feasible. To answer your second question: I would imagine Doug would be invited down if there was reason to believe the plant could be established here."

The girl became all animation, all pink-cheeked excitement. "Daddy, what a grand surprise!" she exclaimed. "Doug deserves a chance, and not just because I'm going to marry him. Doug is a business genius, really he is!"

"The wife of a business genius, my dear, knows when to needle and when not to needle. Is it necessary for me to say more?"

Lois gazed out at the scrappy-cat on the river. Now Eve Barkwell was sailing the last leg of the course that would be used on Race Day. The boat was making good speed, but Lois knew that hers could do better under those same wind and tide conditions. Lois chuckled. "I'll love her in public, Daddy," she promised, "and I'll whup her on Race Day. How's that?"

She could be such a joy to him when she was so warmly happy. His displeasure with her vanished. He gave her hand a squeeze, then strolled back to his library-office to cope with the problem of forcing Miss Eve Barkwell's hand.

Chapter 4

Dissatisfied with her boat's performance in the cross-currents of the Sather River and Town Creek, Eve invited Ken Elston to come for an evening sail in the role of observer and analyst. Ken Elston was flattered. "Talk about a Rockefeller asking for financial advice!" he teased. "When does this interesting inversion occur?"

"Right now, if you'll hustle over here!"

Ken begged for a half-hour in which to dress and bone up on sailing. Actually, it was an hour before his green Pontiac came to a smooth halt before Eve's cottage on Smoke Tree Lane. Eve used the time to good advantage, changing into slacks and a wool shirt, making ham salad sandwiches and a thermos of strong coffee. She stowed the refreshments in her wicker picnic basket and went down the grassy slope to her pier to await Ken. By the time he arrived, she had figured out exactly the course she would sail to give him a good idea of the boat's capabilities. Hardly had he jumped aboard when she got the mooring line cast off and the sail up. She piloted them through the maze of anchored craft in Town Creek and then sailed due north to begin her demonstration where the race would begin, opposite the Sather Yacht Club's big pier.

Ken burbled self-satisfied laughter. "I thought so," he told her. "By an odd coincidence, there stands Miss Lois Hill on the clubhouse porch. One would almost think you take her competition seriously. Why should you?"

"Because the gal is good, for one thing. She knew practically nothing about sailing or this river two years ago, yet I beat her by only two miles. Last year I did it by a mile. And she's spent the winter in Florida, learning to sail a new boat. Add knowledge to basic talent and toss in a good boat for good measure, and I could darned well be licked this year."

Eve brought the boat around in a tight circle and let the boom out to catch all the wind there was. The boat moved forward and gradually built up good speed, but it seemed to Eve that the speed build-up was too slow. "Right there is problem number one," she told Ken. "I've had reports on Lois Hill's *Victory*. I'm told she could run away from me with a following wind like this. All right, you may say, she's always done that and I've always survived. But merely because of superior skill, Ken. Assume she's a far more skilled sailor this year. Well, how would I overcome the big lead she'll probably build up at this stage of the race?"

"Just sail, honey."

It was a grand evening for a long sail. The river and sunset were putting on a grand performance, and the wind held strong and true throughout. Because they were alone on the river, Eve could sail the course she'd decided to sail and use all the tricks she would have used had she been racing under these same conditions.

Once they reached the river, Eve swung to port and commenced the long run toward Kingfisher's Point. The boat surged along powerfully now that it had achieved its best sailing speed. Ken cocked his eyebrows and shrugged. "Nothing wrong with this, you know. Now let me tell you something about the *Victory*. One of the reasons it has good pickup is that its keel is somewhat more rounded and its centerboard is as small and light as permissible. All right. To gain pickup, the designer sacrificed a certain measure of stability. Look. The river is practically calm right now, but Miss Hill certainly couldn't steer as tight a course as this. The *Victory* would yaw."

And he continued to be as optimistic throughout the critical second leg of the course. Indeed, long before they'd reached the buoy near Plaindealing Cove, he predicted flatly that old though she was, the *Vixen* would run away from the *Victory* from that point on.

"All you have to do," he advised, "is limit the lead she'll build up from the starting line to Kingfisher's Point. If that lead is less than half a mile, you'll pass her on this leg and kill her off on the final run home."

Eve wished she could be equally certain. "There's a lot more in all this than meets the eye, Ken," she told him. "Consider. Mr. Hill had the *Victory* built in Maine especially for Race Day. Lois spent the whole winter in Florida, training. Last week when I ran into her in Holloway's Drugstore, she was downright cocky and rude for a while. Why? Why should the Hills make such a project of whupping me on Race Day? And why should Lois be so deliberately rude to me?"

Ken shrugged, a lean fellow of middle height, a strong-jawed, blue-eyed blond who looked as if he'd come to her pier straight from a purveyor of elegant sports attire. For this sail he was attired in pearl-gray flannel slacks, blue, rubber-soled loafers, matching blue gaucho shirt. "Did it ever occur to you," he asked, "that you happen to be rich in a way that Miss Hill would like to be rich?"

Laughter bubbled from Eve; she couldn't prevent it.

"Still," Ken said seriously, "I believe that's the case. Think it over. Lois Hill is dominated by her father. Your father doesn't badger you once in six months. Lois lives a closely controlled life. You live your own life. Lois wanted to be a teacher, but couldn't be a teacher. You wanted to be a watchmaker and you are a watchmaker. You see?"

"Oh, I doubt she's that frustrated, Ken. She travels a good deal, for instance, and travel does please her."

"Anyway, there's my opinion, for what it's worth. You're her rival because you have what she wants. Doubtless she believes she has the edge over you, but until she proves it to her own satisfaction, how can she be sure?"

"If I believed that for an instant, Ken, I'd let her win. This may surprise you, but I rather like her. Care to hear a secret? I pay my apprentice sixty dollars a week. He's worth about twenty-five. Well, from my own pocket I give him a dollar an hour, and Lois Hill makes up the rest."

"Really?"

"Yup."

"But why?"

"Because essentially she's a rather decent girl, that's why. Let me tell you about it. Poor Billy Taylor was sitting on the beach one day when Lois came for a swim. She got to talking with him, as she talks with everyone. He was in a blue mood, and she discovered that he wanted to be a watch-maker but was afraid to hit me for a job. So Lois came into the shop, pretty as you please in her scarlet bathing suit. That was an experience! She proceeded to lecture me on my duty to the un-fortunate, and she proceeded to upbraid me for not having figured out that a crippled fellow needed a sitting-down job such as I could provide. In the end, she talked me into going to him with an offer of training. Last year, to be frank, I paid him only ten dollars a week, which was consid-erably more than he was worth. Lois added fifteen a week to that. Well, when I raised Billy's salary in February, Lois raised him a bit, too."

Eve swung the boat around the buoy near Plain-dealing Cove. The sun had set by then, and the reflection of the nearby trees was long in the water. A bittern took off from the reeds along the shore and was silhouetted prettily for a time against the flame and gold sky. Suddenly it seemed unimportant to finish the demonstration of the *Vixen's* capabilities. Eve eased the boat off from the wind; and then quickly, before Ken could help, she ran the sail down so that they could drift willy-nilly fashion on the current. She opened the picnic basket and tossed Ken a wrapped sandwich. He grinned. "Now how did you know I'm always hungry this time of day?"

"Instinct," she joshed.

They ate and sipped coffee for a time in companionable silence, while the glare left the sky and purple crept over the water. Ken promised suddenly that if she married him, all their long life together would be as peaceful as this. Eve supposed it would be and supposed she would marry him for that reason if for no other reason. The whole thing rather bored her, though. Where was the excitement you were supposed to feel when you met the eyes of the great man in your life? It was all very strange to her; it was all most unsatisfactory. She was positive that if Ken would just yell at her once or if he were less obviously hooked, he would be infinitely more interesting to her. Still . . .

"I had a long talk with my father," Ken told her quietly. "He was upset, of course. It isn't that he thinks a banker's son ought to be able to do better; he isn't a snob, thank heaven. Guess what his primary objection is?"

"I'm content with too little?"

"You're too independent. He cited your battle with the Town Council to prove his point. He said any other person would have been more concerned with public opinion. He said you didn't care a darn about public opinion and that you didn't care who knew it."

"Actually, he's wrong. The folks in this town have always been kind to me. How could I have other than a high opinion of them, and how could I be indifferent to their opinion of me?"

"He said that if I married you and then took over the bank one day, you'd cost me business.

He was quite positive about that."

About twenty feet from the boat, the wing of a barnyard skate broke the smooth surface of the river. Eve hoped for a good look at the creature, for the boat was drifting in that direction. But she never saw it. Ken called: "Sail, ho!" It was the *Victory,* of course, hull flame red against the water, nylon sail full. She had to chuckle. "I think I'm about to be taught a lesson," she said. "If I were a betting girl, I'd bet right now that Lois Hill intends to demonstrate the speed of her boat before the wind."

But the *Victory* came steadily toward them. When she was quite near, Lois dropped her sail to drift along with them. "Not a coincidence at all," she announced cheerily. "Eve, darling, I want to do business with you. When I saw you with your financial adviser, I went home and checked my treasury to make sure I could afford to do business with you."

"Hi, Lois. Or is it to be Miss Hill this April evening?"

"Now don't be squiffy. I despise squiffy people. When we're alone, or practically alone, you may call me Lois. I do vote for the Democrats, after all. I want to purchase your Town Creek holdings. Two thousand an acre for those five acres you're not using."

Eve was caught by surprise.

Lois Hill was amused. "I never thought to see you lose your poise, darling," she commented. "But money is money to those who lack it, eh? Is it a deal?"

"No, I'm afraid not. What surprised me is that the value of that land has shot up a hundred percent in less than a week. I should make more such investments."

"I love Sather, darling. And I do sympathize with you, really, I do. This is an agreeable way out for everyone. You get ten thousand dollars, the town gets land for recreational purposes, and I have the satisfaction of having done something for a town I love."

But her manner changed when Eve said no again. Then and there, lovely Lois Hill had a dreadful tantrum!

Chapter 5

The offer and its refusal tended to embarrass Eve throughout the rest of April. The *Sather Record* publicized the matter, and there were many in Sather who cast Eve in the role of black-dyed villain. None other than Constable Perkins was among these, and he was not averse to telling Eve so, either. He came to her shop on April the thirtieth for that very purpose. He thundered the accusation. He elaborated. "You're the last darned person in town to be so goldanged greedy!" he said. "You want me to remind you of favors folks done for you?"

"Have some coffee," Eve invited. "Billy, pour the nice man some coffee."

"Not if I die of thirst!" Constable Perkins yelled. "Who helped your Pa hundreds of times when he was lying there drunk in the gutter? I'll tell you who. The Women's Club. The Church Sewing Circle. Practically every right-thinking, God-fearing person in town, that's who!"

Eve suggested huskily that he leave.

Constable Perkins sat down instead on the cane-seated chair near Billy's bench. "I ain't proud of reminding you of all that," he said less thunderously. "I ain't proud at all. But what's a man to do when some people forget facts, huh?"

"My father never lay drunk in the gutter, Constable Perkins. My father lay sick in the gutter, and there's a large difference."

"Just the same—"

Eve went on huskily: "And we're discussing different matters. The land is my security. I'm not wealthy enough to give away my security."

"You're offered ten thousand!"

"And it will be worth a hundred thousand some day. Look around you, Constable. Every year more and more wealthy people come to the

Eastern Shore to develop waterfront estates. Good waterfront land is becoming scarce; land within city environs, that is. And it isn't as if my land were the only land available for the Town Council's announced purpose. The Hills have hundreds of acres they don't use. That land is just a quarter-mile upstream from mine. Also, it adjoins Wiley's Anchorage. Why not demand that land?"

"*Demand* it?" He was aghast.

Eve nodded grimly at her bench. "Well, you're demanding mine, aren't you?"

"Well, you ain't Jared Hill."

"Exactly. And for that reason you feel free to come in here to bully me, to insult my father. It must be grand, Constable, to be so brave."

He did have the grace to flush but not to apologize. After he'd gone, Billy Taylor wagged his head. "There's a real mad guy, Miss Eve. Can I tell you something?"

"Certainly."

"Lots of folks are mad at you right now. Sally Peabody was telling me that last night. She said Rod Hatch is stirring everybody up. How come,

Miss Eve? Sally used to think Rod wanted to marry you."

"Who knows; who cares?" Eve asked.

The announcement bells jingled prettily as the door was opened by a young, red-haired fellow Eve had never seen before. He came in with the lordly manner of a fellow who thought he was slumming. He gazed about and pronounced the shop quaint. About to go on in that vein, he had to stop because all the clocks along the walls began to chime the hour. He listened, green eyes rounding. Then he gave a cry of pleasure and strode to the last display counter and leaned on it and studied the antics of the Fifi clock. Atop the white circus horse, the eternally glamorous Fifi did her somersaults, her pirouettes, and her handstands until eleven had been struck. Then Fifi bowed, struck a demure pose and stood still.

The redhead scratched his nose. "I'll have her," he announced. "Your price, miss?"

"I'm afraid she isn't for sale."

He swung about testily. "My dear young lady, everything is for sale. These hands of mine, your skill, this charming performer. Will five hundred be adequate? A thousand?"

Eve smiled and shook her head. "It's always bad luck to sell your heritage, Mr.—"

"Hawkins. Dr. Clifford P. Hawkins, Miss Barkwell. Heritage? What nonsense is that?"

"Not nonsense," Eve said quietly. "My father made that clock for my mother; my mother left it to me. It's quite a remarkable clock, incidentally. Actually, the Fifi has three routines. If you tire of acrobatics, you move the lever a notch and she does a sassy march. Move the lever again, and she becomes a ballerina."

He whistled. "Your father *made* this?"

"Not the music box, of course."

"Could he make one for me?"

"No."

"Is he dead, too?"

Eve decided she'd endured his lordliness quite long enough. "My father is no longer a watchmaker or clockmaker, Dr. Hawkins," she said crisply. "May I help you in any other way?"

"Mind your manners, now! Consider my position! I see a contrivance that amuses me. I offer a sum that must seem quite substantial to you. I'm told that for mawkishly sentimental reasons, the contrivance isn't for sale. I permit that. I then offer to commission the maker to contrive such a clock for me. In what way, young lady, can any of this be offensive to you? I suggest you trot home to bed. Clearly a case of jumpy nerves. Is Dick Hale your doctor? I'll have Dickie pop in on you."

Such a dandy! Such a self-satisfied and regal popinjay!

Eve said, to take him down a peg: "Oh, the girls of Sather will adore you, Dr. Hawkins. Planning to stay long?"

He came grinning to her bench. "Well," he commented, "Lois did say you have spirit, Miss Barkwell. So it goes. You find spirit in the oddest places. Now, then, to business. I wish to buy a watch. Not one of your dull, utilitarian gadgets, mind. Do you find Lois Hill beautiful? So young, so vital! I surprised her once, Miss Barkwell, on a moonlit terrace on Long Island in New York State. Her black hair had such a pretty luster! Laved by moonlight, her bare shoulders and back had the quality, the texture, even, of a gardenia.

Ah, the arrow was shot by Cupid, no doubt of that. But it would seem, Miss Barkwell, that one must first overcome the dubious attraction of a grubber."

"Grubber?"

His green eyes danced. "Ah, I have your sympathy! Very well. I therefore rely upon your good judgment. A pretty bauble, Miss Barkwell. Dick assures me you have an excellent source of supply. Very well. Select me a diamond bauble for Lois, eh?"

"Never diamonds, Dr. Hawkins. Haven't you noticed that Miss Hill wears no jewels? We discussed that once. Miss Hill dislikes display."

"Ridiculous!"

"I'm in business, sir. I would love to sell you the most expensive diamond watch extant. But I can hardly take advantage of a man who relies on my good judgment, particularly if he happens to be a friend of Dr. Hale."

"Did you know it was I who taught Dickie to dig things out of people's eyes?"

"Really?"

"So long ago," sighed Dr. Hawkins, clearly not beyond forty, if that. "We interned, Dickie and I, in a Catholic hospital in New York City. We were in Emergency one evening. There strolled in a female creature with a cubic yard of earth in her left eye. She was related to the Sister Superior in charge, no less, and threatened to tattle if we blinded that eye. Poor Dickie! I had to show him how the work is done."

"He's quite expert now," Eve said, chuckling. "Every now and again he has to dig a filing from my eye."

"What type of watch do you suggest?"

"None."

"Come, come, come!"

"If Miss Hill craves anything, Dr. Hawkins, it's the silver trophy awarded every Race Day to the winner in the scrappy-cat class of boat. Teach her to sail a winning race! All the world is yours, perhaps even the quality and texture of gardenias."

Dr. Hawkins gaped. He met Eve's mischievous brown eyes for fully ten seconds, then exploded into laughter. He laughed up such a storm that

Billy broke discipline for once. Billy actually stopped working to watch and listen frankly.

Dr. Hawkins dragged a chair over to Eve's bench and sat down and studied the disassembled movement on her bench plate. "Interesting trade, yours," he commented. "So much knowledge of things mechanical, so much knowledge of people. Miss Barkwell, I salute you. You're the first person I've met who ever came right out with an offer to accept a bribe to please my Lois. Very well. Name your terms. I'll accept them, and no contempt, I assure you."

"Terms?"

"My dear girl, not if I personally trained Miss Hill for a hundred years could she defeat you and win that trophy. Insufficient stability. I am referring to her, of course, as well as to the *Victory*. Oh, don't argue, please. I, too, have a knowledge of people, a knowledge of boats. Prediction. On Race Day, exciting term, Miss Hill will grab a lead before you've reached the river entrance. Exultant, she'll try to pour it on during the run to Kingfisher's Point. But she'll have too much sail and too tight a course, because she'll become too elated by premature thoughts of victory. Your *Vixen* will plug along and narrow the gap. Come the turn, the run to Plain-dealing Cove. Now you come up fast. Panic! Errors! Then the anger of frustration when you pass her, and deep within her she'll quit long before the race has ended. You see?"

Eve said, shocked: "That's horrible! No person should be so contemptuous of another person."

"Facts are facts, Miss Barkwell. Is a bone a fact? Of course! Then emotional instability must also be a fact. Blame not the observer but the fact."

"At any rate," Eve said warmly, "I'll not throw the race, and I wasn't proposing any such thing."

"Why not?"

"Why not?"

He patted her curly brunette head gently, in fatherly fashion. "Be not proud, Miss Barkwell. All must lose or appear to lose at one time or another. Such a kindness it would be! The dear girl would have her moment in the spotlight; she would have an accomplishment in her history.

Does victory mean so much to you?"

"Of course not."

"There you are. Now you think about it, Miss Barkwell. In the meantime, I shall address myself to the problem of your poor public relations. Mental effort for mental effort, eh? Surely there must be a way for you to keep both your land and the good wishes of your townsfolk. Tonight I shall give fifteen minutes to the little problem."

Eve sputtered: "Are you crazy, Dr. Hawkins?"

"Ask Dickie, there's a good girl."

Eve did, almost the instant he'd left the Clepsydra. Dr. Hale was amused. "Lord, Eve," he said, "I wish I had a dollar for every time I've been asked that question. The answer is no, of course. Actually, Cliff is a world-respected vascular surgeon. Eve, that fellow can insert an inert valve into a blood vessel as easily as you cut a balance staff on that lathe of yours. As for the rest—well, Cliff has always been a nonconformist. Loads of fun, honest, industrious, but different. Has he asked you to dinner?"

"Glory, no!"

"He must be slipping! He has a weakness for brunettes, you see."

"Idiot! He came here to buy jewelry for Miss Hill!"

"Nonsense. When Miss Hill told him of your beauty, right here in my presence, mind, Cliff left charging."

"But he said—"

Dr. Hale asked, laughing: "But doesn't a fellow have to say *something* when he interrupts a girl at her work?"

Eve broke the connection, blushing.

Oh, fine, she thought! She so desperately needed another complication in her badly complicated young life!

Chapter 6

Business and emotional embarrassments not-withstanding, Eve continued to battle the Hills doggedly in the two areas of her incredible competition with them. She replied to the story in the *Sather Record* with a long letter detailing her side of the argument. Miss Elias telephoned a request that Eve withdraw the letter. Eve refused. Miss Elias snapped: "I will not print it." Eve asked, laughing, what had happened to the freedom of the press. Miss Elias stated that the press in Sather *was* free but that she had no intention of being drawn into the ridiculous altercation. Eve pointed out reasonably that Miss Elias should have pondered the inevitable consequences of printing the story Lois Hill had obviously given her. Miss Elias sighed. She asked why in the world she had ever undertaken to write and publish a weekly newspaper in her old age. It was a rhetorical question, though. Miss Elias hung up before Eve could answer it.

Still, the letter was printed. It was effective, too, because Eve had instinctively struck the correct note. Few of the year-round residents of Sather could criticize her, really, for wanting to hold onto her land, because she was Eastern Shore born and bred and wanted to pass that land on to her children one day. Nor could most people argue against her contention that it was unfair to ask her to part with her all when others had hundreds of acres in the same area that they'd really not ever miss. Eve named no names, made no suggestions or proposals. She left it for others to name the names, and the others did.

On Thursday evening, the same day the *Sather Record* printed her letter, the weekly public meeting of the Town Council was nicely stormy. Hardly had Supervisor Wilcox called the meeting to order before young Dorothy Holloway was on her feet, asking how come the Town Council hadn't asked the Hills for land for conversion into public recreational facilities. Supervisor Wilcox gave Dorothy a frigid glare that invited her to sit down. Dorothy didn't sit down. Dorothy swung around and found the face she was looking for. "Miss Hill," she asked loudly, "why are you so interested in paying Eve Barkwell two thousand an acre for her land when you could donate five acres that didn't cost your father six hundred each?"

Supervisor Wilcox declared the speaker and the question out of order.

Chivalry interrupted, in the form of a lanky redhead with mockery in his green eyes and baritone voice.

"My good man," Dr. Hawkins said haughtily, "no speaker and no question are ever out of order in a democratic assembly. The points of this estimable young lady are well taken. An answer by Miss Hill is in order, unless you chance to be a Soviet commissar in disguise."

Eve could have kissed the man!

At once, most people present insisted that the point of any Town Council hearing was to arrive at an informed opinion on the basis of facts, not hearsay. Poor Lois Hill would have beat a retreat, but unfortunately for her, she was trapped in the middle of a long row of occupied seats.

One had to give her credit!

When she rose at last, she was her father's daughter. "I should like to inform Dr. Hawkins," she said clearly, "that a question may be out of order if it is not asked in accordance with established parliamentary procedure. And I would then like to inform Miss Holloway that there is not anything snide in a simple attempt to purchase desired land for donation to the community in which you make your summer home. To clear up any misunderstanding, however, let me explain my position. I understood the town wished those specific acres. I felt the price offered Miss Barkwell was too low. I offered her a fairer price. Is that so snide? My, my! How the dirty rich do grind down the noble poor! And as for land my father could donate: the Town Council wants Miss Barkwell's land. There. Any other questions?"

Eve, moved by genuine admiration, led the applause for the girl. At the same time, she made a mental note to remember that Miss Lois Hill was a rather tough person when she was under pressure. She'd not quit on Race Day, as Ken Elston had predicted. Not that pretty scrapper!

Still, the name having been named and the Hill land having been mentioned, too, the situation at this meeting was quite different from the one that had given Eve a rough time only three weeks before. Dorothy Holloway moved that the Town Council consider the possibility of using Hill land for the announced purposes. The motion was seconded, and despite some hot debate it was carried handsomely.

Elated, Eve headed for the exit. Dr. Hawkins came after her, comically pleased with himself. "I ought to essay politics, don't you think?" he asked. "The correct word, the correct tone—how effective they can be."

He took her arm, presumably because she was a poor frail thing who'd collapse without support.

Eve didn't mind. Out in the purple dusk, she loosed the first sigh of relief she'd been able to loose in days. "I owe you a dinner," she announced soberly. "I doubt the gamble would have worked if you hadn't been there. Dorothy was doing her best, but we both thought that red herring I contrived was too obvious."

"I rather thought it was, Eve. May I call you Eve? Of course I may! I insist it's the duty of a man to establish friendly relations with a young lady as quickly as possible."

"You may call me Eve," Eve told him graciously. "If one may ask, how many of these—er—friendly young ladies are there?"

"One never counts. So ungallant, you know."

Lois Hill caught up with them before they'd gone two blocks.

The girl was having her inevitable reaction to the sudden pressure she'd handled so well. "Cliff," she said crisply, "present your bill and then leave Sather. As for you, Eve: I pledge you here and now that your specific five acres will be acquired by Sather in one way or another."

Quite abruptly, Dr. Cliff Hawkins ceased to be a character. He said with crackling crispness, too: "Does your father die, Lois?"

Already ahead of them, the girl whirled. "You filth!" she snapped.

"No. Merely reminding you that you're not qualified to make certain decisions, young lady. That will be all, thank you."

The girl drew a sharp breath. Eve grinned and said quickly:: "Whoa, there, Lois. You're excited, and you ought to be. Still, I'm the person you hate, not Cliff. Oh, Sir Galahad, may I call you Cliff? Of course I may! I insist it's the duty of a girl to establish friendly relations with a rich young bachelor as quickly as possible."

He was thunderstruck! He was routed!

"Miss Lois Hill," he asked, "May I have the privilege of escorting you home?"

In the end they did go off together, and for a few days Eve was able to forget business and emotional problems and concentrate on the all-important matter of readying herself and her boat for the big race on Memorial Day. On Saturday, with

Ken's help, she got the *Vixen* out of the water and gave it a careful examination from stem to stern. She scraped off barnacles, she splashed on primer. On Monday evening she gave the *Vixen* its first coat of gold paint, and on Thursday evening she stroked on the second coat. In the meantime, she got the latest maps of Town Creek and the Sather River from the Yacht Club library and pored over them millimeter by millimeter until she knew the relative positions of every rock and shoal and sandbar in the course laid out by old Commodore Swanson. Not content to rely upon just the maps, she went to Wiley's Anchorage to check her knowledge against the knowledge of the town's fishermen and oystermen. A good thing she had! Sitting on the deck of Jerry Montague's Hooper Island fantail one afternoon, she asked him if, in a tight race, he would risk hauling up his centerboard and try to skim over Sandbar 162. Jerry paused in the act of checking a trot line. "Where's that?" he asked. When told it lay about a hundred yards that side of the buoy near Plain-dealing Cove, Jerry gave her an odd look. "Let's go for a spin," he suggested. He piloted her over to the Cove, then eased off the buoy to the place where Sandbar 162 was supposed to be. It wasn't there. For good measure, he piloted her over almost every square inch of water within two hundred yards of the supposed sandbar. "What I think," he said finally, "is that they spotted that bar early in the year. But they never last long around here; the water's too fast. Just forget Sandbar 162."

But this race meant too much to Eve to leave anything to chance. The next Sunday she put on old clothes and packed a big lunch and went off for a day of businesslike sailing. The first time around the long course she followed her maps carefully. She sailed as if she were in a race, timing each leg of the course. The second time around she relied upon her own knowledge of the course and made no attempt to avoid Sandbar 162. Her time was much better, a half-hour better, and this despite the fact the wind had dropped somewhat! Encouraged, Eve sailed over to the Yacht Club pier and tied up there to eat her lunch.

Commodore Swanson saw her and came over

for a chat, his shoes squeaking with every step.
"You did that last one in a hurry," he commented.
"Seems to me, Eve, you were taking too many
chances, though."

"Calculated risks, sir. The *Victory* is faster, and
you know it. If I sail conservatively, the *Victory*
will build up a commanding lead. Then all the
pressure would be on me, and if something went
wrong, blooie."

He smiled fondly. "You'll do all right. Taught
you myself, didn't I?"

"Yup. Still, when you're in a race, sir, you have
to do your own sailing."

"How come the hard feelings? Eve, I don't like
that. We've got a good club here. Everybody gets
along, whether he owns a schooner or a scrappy-
cat."

"No hard feelings, sir."

"Huh?"

Eve bit into her second chicken sandwich and
munched away contentedly. When Commodore
Swanson saw that she intended to say nothing
more, he shook his head. "I get the story there's

hard feelings," he said. "That bothers me. So guess what I've been thinking about? I've been thinking maybe we oughtn't to run that particular race."

"Suits me, sir. I have the trophy."

"Yup, you sure do. Funny thing about that. I could've sold myself on betting on the Hill kid last year. The way she made her practise runs, I thought you didn't have a chance. Yet, by golly, you came in a full mile ahead, and loafing along, at that."

"Care to know why, sir?"

"Why?"

"I'm not too proud to assume I can't be licked. Look at me right now! I've sailed these waters for as far back as I can remember. Yet here I am practising, and where is Lois Hill?"

"Practising."

"Where?"

"Over in Cambridge. You ever hear of a handsome young fellow named Doug Chalmers?"

"Nope."

Starboat champ during his college years. Works as a big shot executive for the Hills. Anyway, he came down from Chester in Pennsylvania to give Lois Hill some help. You should've been out here yesterday morning. They did the course three times. Then some of the Hill groundskeepers came with a trailer and lugged the *Victory* away. Secret practise for the next two weeks, I hear tell."

"Gleep!"

Back Eve went to her own practising, and she kept at it the rest of the day until she could barely see to sail her way back to her own pier.

A rugged voice asked: "Honey, why are you so darned stupid?"

Eve flipped her line to Rod, and he drew her in and moored the boat. He helped her up to the pier, and then he gave a strange cry and took her in his arms. "Whoa," she said gently. "Rod, don't you think I'd care if I could? Do you honestly believe I enjoy hurting you, of all people? You're the fellow who lugged Dad home night after night. I couldn't forget that, ever."

"What's wrong with me?"

"Goop. The real question is what's wrong with me?"

He let her go. How could he do otherwise? Nor could he even be angry with her. What was there to be angry about? Not once in all the years he'd known her had Eve been other than honest with him, if not with herself.

"Ah," he said, "stop bawling, Eve! Will you stop bawling?"

Chapter 7

In New York City, feeling sick, Mr. Albert Barkwell sat up on his bed in the William Sloane House Y.M.C.A. and reached again for the last letter he'd received from his daughter. The same old pleas: come home, straighten yourself out, be a man. He hated the words. He'd heard them too often. She was right, but in this case being right didn't matter. It wasn't a question of choice. Things happened, things you couldn't prevent, and there you were. Did she think he enjoyed being a drifter? Did she think he'd not go home if he could?

Knuckles rapped on the door softly. It was the house officer again. Mr. Barkwell told him to come in, and the graying man did. "What's wrong?" the house officer asked. "Is it natural, sir, for a fellow to sit talking to himself?"

"No, it isn't natural."

"We have a house doctor, sir. Look, if money is the problem, forget it. See the doctor now; pay later."

Mr. Barkwell laughed somewhat wildly. "I have a good kid," he said. "You know what she sends me every week? A hundred a week. That's foolish. You have to put something by, because business can't always be good. But it comes every week, wherever I am."

"Nice kid. I could tell you about some kids who aren't so nice."

"She's dead, you see."

"Oh?"

"My wife. You know how it happens, sir? You buy her roses, many red roses. You take them home, and you're happy because spring is in the air and you have a wonderful feeling everything will be all right. Only you never give her the roses. There's the doctor and your crying daughter and your best friends, and nobody says a word, because what's there to say?"

"It happens."

"It happens."

"Not to give you the religious stuff, but did you ever talk it over with your preacher or priest?"

"Can they bring her back to life?"

The house officer sighed and left. He made a call from the house booth down the hall. Presently a stout, puffing man came in with the house officer, and a most peculiar thing happened. The smile on the fat man's face became two smiles, then three, then four. Someone yelled: "Catch him!" Then there was darkness, and then there was light again, but light in a different place, nice golden light that revealed a young woman's face so clearly you could see without trouble some places along her nose where the powder hadn't been smoothed in.

"Powder's tricky stuff," Mr. Barkwell told her. "Use it sparingly, there's a dear, and then give it a final quick swipe with Kleenex."

The woman, whoever she was, blushed prettily.

"Around here," she confided, "they call me Betsie Wrong. I'm always goofing, darn it."

"Why?"

"I don't know. I suppose it's as Sister Alice always says: I move before I think."

"Is this a Catholic hospital?"

"Yup."

"I'm a Protestant."

"We've met them before and will again. Now stop talking, please. Goodness, you've been ill."

"It happens."

"It happens."

"When you buy red roses, you see, and there's no one to take them, lots of things happen."

"To both or just to you?"

"What's that?"

"To you alone, sir, or to your daughter Eve as well?"

"How did you know about my daughter?"

"Well, there you are! Betsy Wrong again, didn't I tell you?"

Mr. Barkwell wanted to think over the implications of her surprising remark, but he grew sleepy again, and so he slept.

His next sensation was that of hunger. He woke up so hungry he felt faint with it, delirious with it. He yelled for food. A nun came in, a great fat one with the reddest and merriest face he'd seen since Santa Claus. "Food there is and food you shall have," the nun said. "But must we shout, sir? Behold, a push button! You push, like this, you count to a hundred, and a nurse comes running or I'll know the reason why."

Oh, but they were generous! *One* soft-boiled egg, *one* slice of toast, *one* cup of tea. The nun watched while he ate. "I always thank God," the nun confessed, "that I'm never ill. Oh, it is a fact you could starve to death on a skimpy dinner like that. But moderation in all things, sir, particularly now, lest other problems be created."

Mr. Barkwell smiled, rather liking her, rather liking this pleasant room with its pale green walls and white trim. He felt oddly comfortable with the warm food sitting well on his stomach. "What happened?" he asked.

"Stupidity, sir. It would appear that you've

neglected to eat. Quite baffling to the Mother Superior, for you had ample money in your wallet. The Y.M.C.A. people of course informed us of a conversation you had with one of their house officers. It was also brought to the Mother Superior's attention by one of our own doctors that you are or have been an alcoholic. Did you know that the skin of a person can reveal addiction to alcohol?"

"I was, Sister. Not any more."

"Fine."

"It was interesting, that. Right after my wife died, I was so busy looking after my daughter that I never thought of drinking. But about a year later, with Eve sixteen and all that, I got to thinking about Helen, and one drink led to another. They used to lug me home, nice guys like Rod and Ken and Jerry. Real nice folks down in Sather. The women of the town sort of looked after Eve without really letting her know they were doing it. Well, that went on four years or so, with things getting worse. Then one evening I got angry with Eve and I slapped. Pretty hard on her nose, I guess, because blood ran. That was when I left

Sather."

Mr. Barkwell stopped, wondering if he'd said too much. It was impossible to tell from the nun's expression. She sat with an unreadable expression, looking not at him but down at her hands on her lap.

"One night," he went on, "I was kicked out of a bar in the Bowery. It was a wet night. The sidewalk was slick with dirt and slime. I guess I must have fallen a dozen times by the time I got to the cheap hotel I was staying in. There was a little mirror in the room, and I saw myself in it, all smeared with dirt and slime, face all red, hair mussed, eyes wild. You know what, Sister? I was shocked. I mean, I was so darned shocked I found the bottle I had in the bureau and I threw it out the window. I haven't touched a drop since."

"Wise, sir. Moderation in all things. Or, as Benjamin Franklin once expressed it: eat not to dullness, drink not to elevation. Why didn't you go home?"

"It's better not to. She's so much like her mother, you see, with those big golden brown eyes and that curly brown hair. I loved my wife very much, Sister."

A nurse came in and said something in a whisper to the nun. The nun nodded and got up. "You mustn't expect me to be impressed by your devotion to your wife, sir," she said. "Letting oneself go, as it were, is hardly congruous with devotion. But we'll talk again when I have more time."

They were all alike, Albert Barkwell thought bitterly. Whether they were nuns or waitresses or fishermen, people were all alike in that they were sure they'd behave differently if they lost someone they loved. He sighed and tried to go back to sleep. But now he felt too wide awake. A picture kept floating before his mind's eye: the face of Eve with blood trickling from her nose, the brown eyes sick with a deep inner hurt. Why had he slapped her? There'd never been a finer girl, a more decent girl, a more amiable girl! All her life she'd been the daughter he'd always wanted. They'd always had such fun together, even in the shop.

An idea occurred to Albert Barkwell. He found

the push button the nun had shown him, and he pressed it once and counted to a hundred. The nurse who called herself Betsy Wrong came in at one hundred and three. He asked for pencil and paper and told her he wanted to write a letter. But when he tried to write the pencil wobbled so in his weak fingers he could make only undecipherable scrawls. The nurse smiled and sat down and told him to dictate the letter to her. Mr. Barkwell dictated: "Dear Eve, I'm much better now in all ways, so no matter what the hospital people write you, don't worry. I think I'll get a job when they discharge me. I love you very much."

The nurse asked: "How come you named her Eve?"

Mr. Barkwell chuckled. "Kid stuff. We wanted three girls and three boys. We named the first girl after the first woman."

The nurse looked at the letter. "Not to be a buttinski or anything like that, Mr. Barkwell, but wouldn't it be better to say these things to Eve? I know I'd rather talk to my father than get a letter from him."

"Well, there's a lot you don't know."

Her blue eyes twinkled. "How can you be sure of that, Mr. Barkwell? You'd be surprised if you knew how much babbling a nurse hears."

He flushed.

The nurse did a surprising thing. She tore the letter into bits. "You think about it, Mr. Barkwell. Then if you still think you want to write a let—"

She broke off, for the stout, red-faced nun was back with the tall, slender, very beautiful brunette who had practically haunted the hospital waiting room for two days. The nurse placed two chairs close to the bed and went out and closed the room door behind her.

It was like being in a dream world again. It was like seeing Helen again as Helen had looked the first day he had set eyes on her. It was like turning the clock back and getting all the sickness and hurt out of his system and being young again and sure that life would always be as glorious as at that very moment. But then—

"Hi," Albert Barkwell said to his daughter.

"Hi, Pop."

"Hi, Eve. I was writing you a letter."

"How are you feeling?"

"Fine."

"You look fine."

"I feel fine."

"I was so worried, Pop. I came as quickly as I could."

"Nothing to be worried about. I feel just fine."

The nun said, "What an interesting conversation!"

They had to laugh, she looked so drolly disapproving. Eve kissed his cheek then, and he gave her arm a squeeze. He used to take her by both arms, he remembered, and pretend he was going to throw her up to the moon. Eve had always liked that game. "Higher!" she used to squeal. Now wasn't it strange that one minute you did such things with a girl, and then the next thing you knew she was a beautiful, grown-up, proper lady actually living in a world that was making serious plans to land human beings on the moon!

Eve said: "You need surgery, Pop. I don't know

what it's all about, but they have to take stones or something out of a kidney."

"Huh?"

"After they told me that, I sent a telegram to Dick Hale. Dick could do the surgery, he answered, but he said it would be foolish of you to travel down to Sather when you're in one of the best hospitals in New York City. What an interesting coincidence! Dick interned here, and so did Dr. Cliff Hawkins."

"I feel just fine. I don't need an operation. What I thought I'd do is take a few weeks to get my strength back and then find a job."

"I'll give you a job. Pop, I have an apprentice, a crippled boy who needs the training and guidance you can give him."

"I don't need charity."

"Goop, it's your shop!"

"Just the same—"

"Young man," the nun interrupted, "of course you'll go home with her after your surgery. If the child is you, she is also your wife. If there is a child, how is there complete mortal death? If there is love, how can there be a complete sense of loss? Rubbish. You've felt sorry for yourself too long. Now say intelligent things to Eve, lest I blister your hide with my tongue."

But words weren't necessary. Eve crinkled her nose at him in the old childish way, and in that moment Albert Barkwell knew that he was going home, and he knew that Eve knew it, too.

Chapter 8

A wonderful thing happened.

While Eve was redoing the living room for the homecoming, her doorbell rang. It was Lois Hill, fetching in blue denims and a short-sleeved yellow cashmere sweater. Lois had all sorts of equipment with her. "I thought I'd help," Lois announced. "In Daddy's company they have a saying that two brains are better than one. I dare say that can be applied to sets of hands."

"What in the world?"

"I don't hate you, you know. It's true that you make me very angry at times, Eve Barkwell, but I don't hate you. It's a sin to hate. Anyway, it stands to reason you can't work here and in your shop at the same time. Even Daddy thinks that. So you tell me what to do and I'll do it. You can poke away at your silly old trade, where you belong."

Eve had to sit down in one of the wicker porch chairs. A cardinal was whistling its fool head off in one of the smoke trees. A mockingbird in an apple tree was mimicking the cardinal with considerable success. There was a nice drone of bees, as well, over in the raspberry patch stretched along the side fence down near Town Creek. On such a grand May afternoon, Eve thought, no one should work; all should sing or just buzz.

"Have a chair," she invited Lois. "Contemplate the wondrous beauty of nature. I never weary of this view. I supose it's dull stuff to a well-traveled girl like you, but it pleases me deeply."

"Oh, I haven't traveled so much. I've never once been to Asia, for instance."

But Lois did sit down, and she relaxed, too, in the warm sunshine. "How's your father?" she asked.

"Operation went off without a hitch. Your Dr.

Cliff Hawkins popped in on him, of all things, and suggested that perhaps Pop ought to spend a couple of weeks more there. Pop couldn't be in better hands. There's a jolly nun there whom Pop likes very much."

"Money?"

"You're very nice, Lois, did you know that?"

"Of course I know that! In fact, if you weren't such a stiff-necked girl, we'd be friends."

"I apologize for my stiff neck."

"Anyway, offering you money doesn't make me or anybody else nice. You just have to do such things, that's all. I mean, if you have more than enough, then you have a moral obligation to help those who may not have enough. That's what Doug always says, and he's right."

"Who's Doug?"

Lois smiled tremulously. "The man I'll marry, I dare say. He's such a fine man. Daddy always says that Doug has his eyes on my loot, but that isn't so. Doug works darned hard, and he's earned every promotion he's had, regardless of what anyone says."

"Works for your company?"

"Yes. And it's a good thing I found Doug, too. There he was just poking along in the hospital sales division! Anyone could tell poor Doug wasn't made to be a salesman! Well, I made Daddy transfer Doug to administration, and it was lucky for the company I did. Now Doug is administrative assistant to the executive vice president, and pretty soon—"

Lois broke off, looking uncomfortable.

"I like your Doug's philosophy," Eve told Lois. "In this case, however, there's ample money. It really wouldn't matter if the bill were five hundred a week."

Lois was puzzled. "You mean your little shop does such a big business?"

Eve nodded. She supposed it morally indefensible to feel so proud of her accomplishment, but proud she was. The Clepsydra had been in the red when her father had signed it over to her three or so years previously. She'd gotten the shop into the black by working fifteen hours a day, doing work not only for her own customers but also for some of the more prosperous shops in Easton. Then had come the opportunity to concentrate upon developing her own clientele. Mr. Bennett of Bennett Jewelers in Philadelphia had had the misfortune to drop his fifteen-hundred-dollar repeater into the river. He'd been so concerned the movement would become rusty he'd brought it to her for emergency measures rather than take it to his own shop in the Chestnut Hill district. He'd been very dubious when he'd discovered a girl at the watchmaker's bench in the Clepsydra. Yet he'd had no choice but to give her the darned thing to clean. He'd stood watching throughout the long process. He'd paid her fifty dollars. A month later, he'd stepped in again and asked bluntly: "Young lady, where did you learn your trade? That repeater has kept perfect time—*perfect* time, mind you—for a month."

"Luck," Eve had said modestly.

"Well," he'd come right back, "let me see what you can do with this job. And I have news for you. It's baffled all nine of my watchmakers."

Actually, the job had been simple for a person

who'd been trained to insert new teeth into train wheels. The watch was a "sticker" only because one of the teeth of the center wheel was a fraction of a millimeter shorter than it ought to be. When the mainspring was almost wound out, there was insufficient force to carry the short tooth of the center wheel through the pinion of the second wheel. Naturally, the watch would then stop. Once a new tooth had been made and inserted, and once the watch had been thoroughly cleaned, the problem was licked. Eight weeks later Mr. Bennett had offered her a supervisory post in Philadelphia. When he had been unable to land her services that way, he'd done the next best thing—signing her to a contract to handle so many jobs a month for a fixed five hundred a month. From then on, the Clepsydra had prospered magnificently.

"Just luck," Eve said to Lois. "Sometimes even tinier shops make good money. If you know your trade and are located in a prosperous area, you can earn good money even in a barber-shop window."

The telephone rang in the living room. A pleasant voice asked for Lois, and Lois rushed to the telephone. Eve climbed back up on the stepladder to continue the renovation of the ceiling. She stuck her roller into the tray of yellow KemTone and got a couple of feet of the ceiling covered before Lois said: "I'm busy dear," and pronged the handset.

"That was Doug," Lois announced. "He has to go to New York next week, and he wondered if he couldn't bring your father back to Sather with him."

"Wonderful!"

"You understand, don't you," Lois asked, "that none of this makes any difference insofar as the race and the land question are concerned?"

"Oh, absolutely!"

"There are some things a girl just has to do, you see. It isn't even a question of hating you or wanting to embarrass you. A Hill just has to meet all challenges."

"Fine."

"I could do that painting. In Paris last year I painted my mother's ceiling with a roller."

Eve promptly got down and waved the girl up. Although she had little at the shop that needed attention, she humored Lois by changing and by leaving as if to deal with urgent business.

Billy, Lord love him, was working quite as industriously as if she were standing over him with a whip. He was doing a Hamilton pocket watch, handling each part with loving care because he had a downright passion for Hamiltons. "Mr. Elston was in," Billy told her. "Mr. Elston Senior, that is."

"State his business?"

"Something about land, Miss Eve. He said if you'd drop in to see him, he'd appreciate it."

"Need anything; want anything?"

"I could use a sandwich, thanks. Golly, the chow I've been eating lately! Sally, she says I'll get fat around the middle like all other crippled guys if I'm not careful."

"She's right. What you need is less food and more exercise."

But Eve bought him a sandwich in Holloway's before she went to the bank.

Senior received her jovially, waving her to a chair, asking about her father, offering to help her in any way he could. But he was not a man to spend much time on preliminaries when he had business to conduct, and he had business to conduct this day.

"Eve," he said growlingly, "the Town Council has appointed me chairman of a new committee to be called the Sather Development Committee. No pay is involved, of course. And along with the appointment I've received a headache, it would seem. I refer to the land question. Now, then, it seems to me there's been too much emotion in all this and too little common sense. I take pride in the fact that I generally apply common sense to all business matters, and I shall try to apply common sense here. Specifically, what are your objections to the proposed recreational area?"

"None. I'm all for it, in fact. I do object, though, to the utilization of my land for that purpose."

"Ideal location."

Eve chuckled. "That's a matter of opinion, sir.

After all, what is an ideal location? In these parts there must be access to water, of course. Well, the Hill land lies along Town Creek. Other land lies along either Town Creek or the Sather River."

"Still, someone must form an opinion and then act on the basis of that opinion. I've looked into the situation rather closely, Eve, and I'm of the opinion that your land is what we want. Now, then, I do think you're justified in wanting a fairer price. Frankly, if I owned that land I'd not accept less than three thousand an acre. I have told Supervisor Wilcox this. While he personally felt a thousand an acre was enough, he did submit the matter to the others on the Council, and they've agreed that three thousand per acre ought to be paid. Acceptable?"

"No, sir."

"Come, come, Eve. Never make decisions that quickly. Consider everything before you make business decisions."

"I was more or less told that the night I turned down a thousand an acre, sir. Now I'm offered three."

He frowned. "Oh, I see. Very well. Suppose you name your price, and we'll proceed from there."

"Fifteen thousand an acre, sir, and an assurance in black and white that the land will never be used for other than recreational purposes. After all, my home adjoins that land. I'd not want a factory thumping away next door."

"Are you serious?"

"Yes, sir."

"My dear young lady, not even land fronting Morris Street will bring more than five thousand an acre."

"One day it will. In my lifetime, too. Sir, I think that's the point you fail to grasp. I'm twenty-three. I bought my land for investment purposes. I'm young enough to carry it for many years. It will be land to turn over to my children. Perhaps by the time they're grown, each of those acres will pay for a complete college education for a child."

"Ridiculous!"

"I paid five hundred an acre not too long ago,

sir. Now I'm offered three thousand an acre. A fantastic increase in value already. How, then, can you claim my thinking is ridiculous?"

The point was so well taken that he abandoned his argument. "Well, let me put it this way," he growled. "The land isn't worth that price now, and the Town Council won't have to pay it. If need be, the Town Council will exercise the right of eminent domain. The matter will then be referred to court. The court will appoint a referee to determine the land's true value. Whatever that value is, the Town Council will have to compensate you to that extent; not a penny more, not a penny less. I would hate to invoke eminent domain, though. Frankly, many of our people would disapprove. They'd feel you were being bullied."

"I'd do my best to encourage them in that thought, Mr. Elston. And, of course, I'd also ask the court to determine if mine is the only land the town can use for the purpose. In other words, sir, I'd force the town to grab the land for that stated purpose. Then if the land were used for a business enterprise, say, I'd sue on the grounds it was obtained from me fraudulently."

He smiled faintly. "What do you think you know, Eve?"

"I think I know that the land is mine, sir. What else is there to know?"

He sighed. "Well," he said, "I do hope you know what you're doing."

Chapter 9

But it wasn't to be. The following week none other than Dr. Cliff Hawkins came to the shop and invited Eve to come for a drive with him. Eve told him warmly that she wasn't a brilliant surgeon who could afford to loaf whenever she chose. Cliff winked at Billy Taylor. "Young fellow," he asked, "wouldn't you say there's a dreadful case of nerves here? Come, Miss Barkwell; we're wasting time."

Eve yielded grudgingly. "One hour," she told him. "Not a minute more."

It proved to be a full afternoon's ride, however. The redhead popped her into his Thunderbird and drove her north to the dairy farm area, just ambling along at about fifteen miles an hour so that the cattle and the lush pastureland could be fully seen and appreciated. "The wretched news first," he announced. "It occurred to me after earnest conversation with your father that his return to Sather would be a mistake. One is hardly ever wrong, of course, but on the off chance I might be in this particular case, I took the liberty of consulting several psychologists with whom I work from time to time. They concurred in my opinion. It therefore amused me to find your father a suitable post in New York City."

Eve stared at him incredulously.

"Consider," Cliff Hawkins ordered. "Regardless of extenuating circumstances, your father did touch bottom here. Further, the house he would live in is the house in which your mother died. Now I ask you! Is this the time to remind the man of other days, a happier way of life? It seemed dangerous to me and to the psychologists. One must move forward always. And you may as well know your father was relieved when I announced I'd found him a post in New York."

"But he promised! I was counting on him!"

"The promises of the ill are never binding. And what were you counting on him for? Rubbish. My dear girl, I would say you're the least dependent creature I've met in years. You appear entirely adequate in all the ways that count. Would you have the man retrogress at the very moment he shows improvement?"

Eve asked, startled: "Cliff, do you seriously believe he would?"

They came to a pretty little creek meandering along through a peach orchard. Birds were everywhere, and there were even two turkey buzzards floating about on still wings high in the powder blue sky. Noticing Eve's interest in the scenery, the elegant doctor stopped the car in the shade of a newly leafed maple. "To answer your question," he said soberly, "I think it important that your father develop a new life in a city such as New York. In that city he is but one of millions of men. Here, he'd be a marked man. I'd let him toil away for a year or two—find himself, so to speak—before I brought him back."

"Billy will be so disappointed! Just the thought of working under a genius like my father made Billy a very happy boy."

"One must rise above these petty disappointments," Cliff said. He chuckled. "Interesting. I said the same thing only this morning to Mr. Hill. That distinguished gentleman was intent upon returning to headquarters to supervise some grubby merger or other. He was not joyous when I forbade it. So it goes. Into each life some rain must fall, and all that."

It took Eve a good ten minutes to cope with her disappointment. He was quite patient with her, just sitting there smoking and watching the antics of the birds. Presently, after she'd nodded and shrugged, he drove on again, cutting back to the river and following the water three or four miles toward the confluence of the Sather and the Choptank. When they reached the hamlet of Jowett, Cliff parked near the water's edge and gazed about the Sather as if looking for something. Finally he spotted a sail off to their left, and he chuckled. "Miss Lois Hill returns, fully trained to race," he said. "I find all this quite amusing, incidentally. I've known the family for three years. This is the first time I've known Lois to subject herself to the rigors of discipline. A head must roll! Yours, to be precise. And why? You bring out the competitor in Lois, that's why."

Eve watched the *Victory* with interest. Lois was tacking upstream, exactly as she would have to during the second leg of the race on Memorial Day. And Lois wasn't just loafing along, either. Actually, she was sailing right now as if she were in a race, and she was doing a creditable job, too. But every so often the boat would slip off the wind somewhat, and the sail would luff, and there would be no forward progress to speak of. The girl was learning, but she'd really not yet learned enough. If her lead during the first leg were held to a minimum, Lois would be out of the race before they'd sailed half the second leg.

"Do you perceive what I perceive?" Cliff Hawkins asked.

"I'm afraid so."

Her comment surprised him. "Afraid?"

"Well, isn't it a pity, Cliff, to train so hard so uselessly? It isn't fair, in a sense. Actually, Lois shouldn't be entered in my class. She has by far the better boat, but just for dashes before the wind. I could lick her if I were sailing the *Victory*, sure, but it would take all the know-how I have."

"Doug Chalmers has bet her father a thousand to a hundred that Lois will defeat you by at least ten lengths."

Ridiculous!"

"The statement was made after he'd watched you practise the other afternoon."

Eve grinned. "Mr. Chalmers will be disappointed, I'm afraid. It's a silly girl who displays all her tricks during a practise session anyone can watch."

By easy stages, they trailed the *Victory* back to Town Creek in Sather. Cliff parked on the Yacht Club grounds and took Eve across the little bridge to Wiley's Anchorage to welcome Lois Hill home from her training session. "Delightful sailing," he assured Lois. "And what ever happened to the estimable Doug?"

"You shut up!"

"Temper!"

Lois looked at Eve, exasperated. "Darling," she asked, "will you please stop encouraging this creature to come down here? Really, Cliff, you could have been kinder to my father."

"Why? His health is either good or less than good. He pays me to give him the facts. The fact is that he ought to divest himself of his business interests. He knows it, just as I know it. What to do? Why, tell him the facts over and over again until he bases his actions upon them."

Lois clambered out of the *Victory*. She gestured to an attendant. "Complete overhaul for the race," she ordered. "Do a good job, mind you."

He saluted crisply.

Lois gave him two twenty-dollar bills and stretched in the warm sunshine. Her gray eyes glowing, she said: "It was a lovely sail home. Oddly enough, I enjoyed every minute of the tacking. The *Victory* responded so very beautifully. I actually got the feeling, Eve, that you'll be out of the race before it's half over."

"I doubt it."

"Naturally."

A horn beeped in the parking lot of the Anchorage. Lois looked toward a white convertible Cadillac and waved vigorously. A big fellow got out and came toward them, a joltingly handsome fellow with a squarish face and very keen blue eyes.

Lois took his left hand most possessively. "Coach," she said, "meet the opposition. Miss Eve Barkwell, may I present Mr. Douglas Chalmers?"

"Happy to meet you," Eve said.

"Delighted, Miss Barkwell. I'm looking forward to the race, needless to say. You handle a boat quite well."

"Or I'm luckier than I ought to be, Mr. Chalmers."

"Or would have us believe it's all luck, eh?" He chuckled. It was a stirring chuckle, so boyishly infectious and so warmly male that Eve had to chuckle with him.

"Ginger ale?" Lois asked. "That trip left me thirsty."

Eve remembered she still had some work to do

and shook her head. Cliff Hawkins, of course, promptly scolded her once they got back to his Thunderbird. "Must you be stupid?" he asked. "One ought to be more clever. Dear girl, it was my thought that over ginger ale or something you could uncover their race strategy."

"Why do you care, Cliff?"

"Why wouldn't I care? Was I born to the purple? No. Therefore, I sympathize eternally with the underdog. Do you own a specially built boat? No. Do you possess a sailing champion as coach? No. Do you receive a world tour if you win? Again, no. You see?"

"A race is just a race, Cliff. Even if I lose, it won't matter."

"Care to know, dear girl, how important this victory is to Lois? It's been implied, merely implied, mind, that she would almost meet your ridiculous price for that land if she were to win that race."

"Really? But why?"

"As I've said before, dear girl, you have so much of what she craves. But if she were to defeat

you, then some sort of balance might be struck.
People are that way, you know. Into each life
comes a person to plague you. You plague her. Do
you kowtow to the rich? No. Do you humor the
sweet thing? No. Do you lose races to the sweet
thing? No. Do you yield land to the sweet thing?
No."

It was food for thought. Eve digested it that
evening after a lonely dinner in her cottage near
Town Creek. And she had an odd thought, there
on her porch. She wondered just what would happen if she so contrived things so that Lois Hill
would win after a nip and tuck battle on Race
Day. What would the loss matter to a girl who
sailed for pleasure? There'd be talk for a few days,
but that would be all. And if Lois were to strut a
bit, so what? You had to remember there was a
wonderful side to the girl's character. The girl was
helping Billy, and the girl had come to her to offer
free transportation home for the convalescent. The
truth was that Lois didn't hate her even a little
bit. Lois was just enough of a Hill to hate defeat,
that was all. So if she were to know a victory . . .

But there the thinking stopped. Doug Chalmers parked the Cadillac before Eve's fence. He got out, waved. He gave a quick look around as he approached the porch. "Very nice," he said. "You have a vest pocket estate here, Miss Barkwell, haven't you?"

"You're very kind, Mr. Chalmers. Won't you sit down, please?"

He did. He gazed at the land beyond the right-hand side fence. "I take it," he said, "that yonder is the land in question?"

"It swings around my back fence and comes down to the creek," Eve told him. "It's coveted, really, because it's rather isolated from this residence area."

"Mr. Hill has put me on the matter," he announced. "It seems to mean a great deal to him. You'd not make my job easier, would you, and accept three per acre?"

"No, sir."

"Do you know what it is, I wonder, to come into conflict with a tiger of industry? Unless one has immense resources, frustrating a tiger is a foolish thing to do."

"Actually, I'm not trying to frustrate Mr. Hill. I simply want either the land or seventy-five thousand dollars for the children I hope to have one day."

Creases appeared in his forehead. "Isn't that an unusual concern, Miss Barkwell? I mean, this concern about the welfare of children you don't have?"

"I don't think so, Mr. Chalmers. Most people who've been through the mill want their children to have easier lives. I've worked as much as eighteen hours a day. It isn't pleasant, as I suspect you know."

He shrugged. "No, it isn't pleasant. Still—"

"What does Mr. Hill want the land for, Mr. Chalmers?"

"Why, to give to the town!"

Eve said gently, "I rather doubt that, sir. Why would you be in the matter, in that case? I'm sure there are other things you can do for the company."

"Mr. Hill has a heart problem, Miss Barkwell.

In a sense, he's also committed to get that land for Sather. So, reasonably, he's brought me into the case. But to get to the important thing: I'm to buy it or smash you. You seem a nice person, so here I am to spare you pain. Shall I give you the check?"

"Nope."

A disturbing thing happened. The tough, handsome man said: "It's your neck, then," and got up and left.

Chapter 10

The big day broke clear and gusty. Eve knew even before she got out of bed that it was the type of day she would have selected had she been given the chance. The wind whistled along the eaves of her cottage and made her television antenna hum atop the roof. When she went outdoors after a light breakfast of poached eggs, she saw whitecaps on Town Creek and all the trees tossing. It seemed to her as she walked to Wiley's Anchorage that she ought to defeat Lois Hill by three miles this Race Day, and she found others en route who agreed with her. Rod ambled over from his gasoline station, wagging his head. "The Hill girl doesn't have much luck, does she?" he asked. "Funny thing about that. The news we got last night was that we'd have her kind of weather down here—light breezes, smooth water."

"So it goes," Eve said easily. "Actually, she really ran out of luck when she had that boat built up in Maine. Maine people may know boats, but they don't necessarily know Eastern Shore weather. They should have built an all-round boat for her."

Rod hesitated, then shoved out a grimy hand. "Good luck, Eve. Maybe we squabble too much and maybe we don't see eye to eye on the land matter. Just the same, I want you to win."

"Did you think I didn't know that, goop?"

A couple of blocks later, Eve found none other than Doug Chalmers obviously waiting to waylay her. An odd thing happened to her. There came a jolt. She met those keen blue eyes, and they warmed her strangely, and then it was as if she had walked into a brick wall.

"Good sailing weather for starboats," he commented. "I imagine your scrappy-cats will have a difficult time, though."

"Not really, Mr. Chalmers. You sail a bit more conservatively, that's all. At least I will."

"Lois will, too," he said grimly. "Frankly, though, I came to ask a courtesy. Lois's father is a bit worried. He finally got Lois to agree to ask for a postponement if you would."

"Fine with me. Why not? This is a race, not a life-or-death matter. Only trouble is, the Board of Governors won't postpone. That's in the rules, I'm afraid."

"But surely if both you and Lois asked—"

Eve chuckled; she couldn't help it. "We're just two of twelve racers in that race, Mr. Chalmers. I think that's something you and too many others have forgotten. Everyone assumes it's between Lois and me. But we have some darned good sailors and darned good boats entered against us. Glory, why do you think I've trained so diligently? Did you think I was training just to defeat Lois?"

"If you ask for a postponement, others will follow your lead."

Knowing it was silly, Eve did request a postponement just to please him. Commodore Swanson was outraged. "You know the rules," he snapped. "It's today or next year."

Eve looked at Doug Chalmers and shrugged. He got the point and sighed and went over to Wiley's Anchorage with her to give Lois the bad news. Lois, surprisingly, wasn't a bit disturbed. "Told you so," she said briefly. "Anyway, the *Victory* can handle any weather, and the *Vixen*, too."

Eve wished her luck and went over to her own boat. She slipped into it and got the sail up and headed for Town Creek. She fiddled around at the far end of the creek for the next half-hour, testing the boat's response to hard shoves on the tiller and to demands that it sail very close to the wind. Everything went as well as she thought it would. The *Vixen* might not be the loveliest craft in the race, but she was Eastern Shore built, and she handled the rough waters and the gusty wind with aplomb. Indeed, when the starting gun was fired at eleven o'clock sharp, the *Vixen* shot forward as if to demonstrate once and for all that she was swift as well as seaworthy. Even though the *Vic-*

tory broke beautifully from the starting line, the *Vixen* held her own almost to the mouth of the Sather River, and once they had swept around the buoy into the river, the *Vixen* closed fast. Lois was dumbfounded. She gave a startled cry and let her boom out so that her nylon sail could get all the wind there was. The stratagem worked, but only for a limited time. After the *Victory* had grabbed a twenty-foot lead, it began to heel before the too heavy wind. Eve, sailing more conservatively and taking advantage of her bigger centerboard, came abreast of Lois as Lois pulled in her boom to slip some wind.

But Lois was a quick learner, darn it! Lois set her sail as Eve had set hers and was content to let the difference in the boats decide the issue during the first leg of the race. The *Victory* inched ahead until clear water lay between the two boats. Eve tried to force a second mistake by letting her boom swing wider, but even though she narrowed the lead somewhat, Lois stuck to her conservative sailing. Once Eve had to slip the wind herself, the *Victory* regained the distance it had lost and then proceeded to add to its lead. Back there came to Eve a Hill yell of exultation.

Eve went back to conservative sailing, too. She sailed along calmly, not bothering even to measure the lead Lois was building up en route to the first turn-around buoy near Kingfisher's Point. She was content to watch Lois make the turn about twenty lengths ahead, and from the technique Lois used to make the turn she picked up some useful information. She noticed that Lois, who had swung around tightly, had to duck in a hurry to avoid being decapitated by her boom. While Lois wallowed in the rough water, trying to get up headway again, Eve made a very wide swing-around, easing gradually to take the wind on the starboard. She made up ten lengths before Lois got up headway again, and from that moment on it was Katy bar the door!

A good half-mile in the lead by the time the *Vixen* neared Plain-dealing Cove, Eve came to the conclusion that this was one time when perhaps it might be well to rub it in. So instead of skirting Sandbar 162, as listed in the race orders, she ran over the place where it was supposed to be and picked up another quarter-mile lead while Lois was dutifully sailing wide of the danger spot to avoid disaster. And now, as if scenting triumph, the old *Vixen* took all the wind gave it and bowled along back toward Town Creek. The lead became a mile, a mile and a half, two miles. By then, deciding that she'd made her point, Eve drew her boom well in and was content to loaf the rest of the way to the finish line. She eased over the line, waved deliberately to Mr. Jared Hill and Doug Chalmers on the Yacht Club pier, and then sent the *Vixen* back to Wiley's Anchorage.

Big Moe gaped at her as she eased into her berth at the contestant's pier. "Hey," he yelled, "you got a motor in that thing?"

Eve tossed him the line. He pulled her in and held her steady while she dropped the sail and wound it about the boom.

"Kiddo," he asked, "did you take a short cut or something? Everybody said this would be the slowest race in years."

"Rubbish, Moe. The *Vixen* just felt her oats,

that's all. Did you see the old girl battle the *Victory* even almost to the river? Imagine!"

Dorothy Holloway came racing over, whooping and cheering as if they were still with the Pep girls of old Sather High. "Honey," Dorothy squealed, "dinner's on me! I don't care whether you want filet mignon or roast whale, I'm buying!"

"Roast whale," Eve chose. She climbed nimbly to the small pier. From that coign of vantage she had a clear view of Town Creek and of the crowds lining both shores. She noticed that practically no one had left and that practically everyone was looking toward the river, apparently waiting to see how badly beaten Lois Hill would react to her defeat.

Moe asked worriedly, "Did you have to pour it on, Eve? I was watching from the river shore. You had her licked good by the middle of the second leg. Why rub things in like that?"

"Strategy."

"What strategy?"

"Very simple. Moe, the real battle between Lois and me wasn't this race. For reasons best known to herself, she's decided that my land will be picked up one way or another. So it occurred to me out there that perhaps if I gave her a real licking, she might be a bit nervous about tangling with me again. Silly thought and silly hope, perhaps, but all one can do is think out a course of action and then do her best."

Now the *Victory* came into sight, and Eve had to admire Lois Hill, because the girl was sailing all out, quite as if she were determined to make the best finish possible. Half crouching in the stern of the *Victory,* eyes straight ahead despite some admiring cheers, Lois drove the *Victory* hard across the finish line, then at once swung it in toward the Yacht Club pier.

"Good kid," Eve said sincerely. "Dorothy, how come we don't make her a friend? Glory be, why are we always arguing with her?"

"Please," Dorothy begged, laughing, "no emotion. The trouble with that girl is that she turns on you quick as a cat. Well, shall we go collect that trophy again? It's becoming a bore, you know. They ought to give you the darned thing permanently and then disqualify you from further competition."

With Moe happily leading the way, they followed the half-dozen catwalks across the Anchorage to the little bridge leading to Yacht Club property. Moe made room for them with expert weavings of his big shoulders as people crowded in to inform Eve they'd known all along she'd keep the trophy down on the Eastern Shore, where it belonged. But all the congratulations and handshaking ended when they entered the Yacht Club's main building. In the big lounge, Lois Hill was jabbering away heatedly with Commodore Swanson and several members of the Board of Governors. And right there, jabbering away with her, was none other than Doug Chalmers.

Doug Chalmer's words stopped Eve cold. "The fact remains," he snapped, "that a foul was committed by Miss Barkwell. You can argue the matter from now until eternity, gentlemen. You can claim from now until eternity that Miss Barkwell had a commanding lead at the time the foul occurred. Still, a foul was committed, and whatever hope Miss Hill had of catching Miss Barkwell was dashed by that foul. Read your own rules! Your own rules state a competitor must be disqualified if the course isn't followed correctly. Read them!"

Moe yelled: "Hey, are you calling Eve a cheat?"

Moe started for Mr. Doug Chalmers as if he intended to stamp him to death. Eve nipped between the men. "Whoa," she told Moe, "whoa."

Tears in her eyes, her face white, her whole body trembling, Lois grabbed her by the arm. "You miserable cheat!" Lois cried. "A big lead wasn't enough, was it? You had to make so terribly sure of humiliating me, didn't you? You had to cheat, didn't you?"

Eve looked at Commodore Swanson.

"Miss Hill claims," he announced, "that you didn't swing west around Sandbar 162, Eve. Says you sailed right over it and picked up a good quarter-mile on her."

"Right."

"Well, there you are," Doug Chalmers said. "It isn't even necessary to wait until the umpires come over, Commodore. Miss Barkwell herself admits she fouled."

Eve whirled on him. "How did I admit that, Mr. Chalmers?"

"Why, Miss Barkwell, the rules of the race quite specifically state a contestant will be disqualified if the course isn't followed correctly. The race instructions specifically state each contestant is supposed to skirt each sandbar and not gamble there's enough water over any one to carry the craft across without mishap. Right?"

"Right. Only there isn't a sandbar there."

Commodore Swanson gaped. "Sure there's a bar, Eve. Ask anybody."

"Ask the fishermen, sir. I sailed that area both in the *Vixen* and aboard Jerry Montague's fishing boat. We never could find that bar, and you can't, either."

Doug Chalmers grinned. "According to the race officials, Miss Barkwell, there is a bar there. The maps showed it, and you were technically required to skirt it. Lois did. Lois obeyed every rule of the race, and because she did, she lost her chance to catch you on the third leg, as planned."

"Not in a million years, Mr. Chalmers."

"How do you know?"

It was Mr. Swaisland who asked the question, a little man whose interest in things nautical ended this side of the water's edge. He shrugged and went on: "I've always heard it said, Miss Barkwell, that a race isn't over until the finish line has been crossed. It's always possible, it seems to me, that you could have had a mishap or that the wind could have shifted. In any event, I must say that whether the maps were in error or not isn't the question here. The maps did show the sandbar, and the rules do require that all indicated sandbars be skirted. By your own admission, then, you did commit a foul, and by that admission, of course, you compel me to disqualify you and declare Miss Hill here the winner."

Moe yelled: "Boy, what a lousy technicality! Boy, what a way to win a race!"

"Fair's fair!" Lois Hill screeched. "It is so!"

Along about then Eve began to suspect that the situation was hopeless. Still, she had to say something, so she said it. "Commodore," she said, "if you disqualify a racer for not avoiding a non-existent sandbar, you'll be the laughingstock of the Eastern Shore. I never once sailed out of bounds, as the umpires will tell you. I never once took a foolish chance. Now you can declare Miss Hill the winner, naturally, but you'll never convince even yourself that I licked her by two miles because I didn't skirt that nonexistent bar."

But what could Commodore Swanson do, with Mr. Swaisland insisting on a strict interpretation of the rules and with the two other members of the Board of Governors siding with Mr. Swaisland and Lois Hill?

Eve said sweetly to Lois: "Congratulations on your brilliant victory, Miss Hill. Next time we race, I'll bring a tongue to win for me, too."

Lois went livid.

Eve nodded pleasantly to Doug Chalmers, then turned and left.

Chapter 11

A dreadful thing happened. Practically the entire town of Sather boycotted the Yacht Club Presentation Ball. A couple of fishermen actually made great jeering signs and picketed the grounds until Constable Perkins threatened to jail them if they didn't cease and desist. Inasmuch as either of the fishermen could have broken the constable in two without effort, all the fellows laughed. After they'd booed Lois Hill's arrival, they tossed their signs into Town Creek. When Lois was finally awarded the trophy in the great candlelit ballroom, there were only three or four on hand to applaud.

Worse, Miss Elias stated her opinion of the whole matter in the following week's edition of the

Sather Record. She asked if it weren't time for Race Day to be dropped from Sather's schedule of vacation events. She submitted that when a big race could be won in the Yacht Club rather than out on the water, the whole thing lacked meaning. She further submitted that the Yacht Club had been ill-advised to award the victory to Lois Hill simply because Mr. Swaisland, manager of the Hills' Eastern Shore farms, no less, had elected to interpret the rules with ridiculous strictness. "One wonders," Miss Elias wrote, "if the rules would have been interpreted so strictly had Lois Hill sailed over the nonexistent sandbar. One makes no accusations. One simply states that Mr. Swaisland could hardly have been impartial, and then one leaves it to the reader to draw his own conclusion."

War!

In the next issue of the *Sather Record* appeared a full-page announcement authored by Mr. Swaisland. He stated that without rules there could be no competition worthy of the name. He stated that he remained convinced Miss Hill *might* have caught Miss Barkwell had Miss Barkwell skirted the sandbar, too. And he then stated that the poor sports were Eve Barkwell and the townspeople who had denied Miss Hill the satisfaction of receiving her trophy under the same circumstances Miss Barkwell had received hers two years in a row. For the town of Sather, Mr. Swaisland publicly apologized to Lois Hill.

War!

The next paid announcement was inserted by Moe of Moe's Diner. He announced that the town of Sather would put on a grand presentation ball any day in the week Miss Hill demonstrated she could not be beaten by Eve Barkwell by more than half a mile. "What I object to," Moe then went on, "is that a paid employee of the Hills was allowed to take the victory from Eve."

The blast drew blood, or a reasonable facsimile thereof. Mr. Swaisland came to the Clepsydra, fire in his eyes. "You behind this announcement?" he asked Eve. "Yes or no?"

"No."

"Any more stuff like this, and I'll sue. I'm not a kid. I've got my pride. When I hire out to work for a man, I don't sell my honor. I'd have called the same foul on Lois Hill, and you know it."

"I really don't know that, sir, since frankness seems indicated. I would hope you'd be fair under those circumstances. But who knows?"

He slammed the newspaper onto the counter. He stood there rigidly for perhaps a minute, and then he asked: "You think a two-bit shopkeeper is going to get the best of the Hills? You're barking up the wrong tree. Sure, you could've beaten her that day, and I guess you could beat her any day she races you. But that isn't the point. You fouled. It was a goof, sure. Even Lois Hill and Doug Chalmers knew that. And if you'd been a good sport and attended that ball, Lois would have said so. Instead—"

"What did Commodore Swanson say, Mr. Swaisland?"

"What difference does that make? He's only one member of the Board of Governors."

"That was why the ball was boycotted, sir. Everyone knows and loves Commodore Swanson. Had he called the foul, that would have been that."

Mr. Swaisland growled and stalked out.

But that wasn't the end of the matter. That same evening none other than Mr. Elston came to the cottage down near Town Creek. Mr. Elston looked the place over and pronounced it the prettiest place in town. "You know what?" he asked. "I think my son chases after you because he wants to live in a pretty place like this."

"We're just friends, sir. Surprise! I have several good male friends. There's Rod. There's Ken. I've even acquired a red-haired doctor of late. But you notice, sir, don't you, that I wear no engagement ring, even though I could pick one up for an admirer at cost?"

He studied her winsome, dimpled face. "How come?"

"I blame my father, sir. He trained me to be entirely self-sufficient. Most fellows resent self-sufficient women. Or shall I tell you the truth? I like them and they like me, but I don't love them and they don't really love me."

"Rod?"

Eve considered her hands on her lap. "You must remember," she said carefully, "that Rod and I were sweet on one another in high school. But you grow up; you develop different interests."

"Not Rod. In fact, to be frank, Ken's interest in you has always troubled me, because I've seen you with Rod many times. Call me old-fashioned, but I never did care much for women who play the field."

"At least you're frank," Eve said, smiling. "Care for coffee?"

"I'd better not have any. But while we're being frank, let me say frankly that something is happening in this town that disturbs me. I don't like this animosity that's being shown the Hills. Other wealthy summer people rather dislike it, too. The trouble with a thing like this is that it can get out of hand. The first thing you know, you build a wall between summer people and year-round people. Then the town isn't a nice town any more."

Eve said hotly: "I've said nothing, I've written nothing."

"Commodore Swanson tells me you resigned

from the yacht club on June fifteenth."

"Of course."

"He also tells me that about fifty other persons resigned shortly thereafter."

"What would you expect, sir?"

"Well, what's the point of resigning? Is it your intention to wreck the club? That can be done, you know. It's the year-round people who actually support it. But what's the point of wrecking one of the few tourist attractions we have?"

"My intention was to protest an unfair action, sir. Actually, each of the arguments made that day was a good argument. In one sense I did break a rule, because the sandbar was indicated on the maps. In another sense I didn't break a rule, because I never sailed out of bounds and I never sailed *over* a sandbar. The thing should have been adjudicated after suitable study, and certainly after an appraisal of the actual effect of the so-called violation upon the outcome of the race. But Mr. Swaisland, who certainly wasn't a disinterested observer, came to a lightning decision and spoke so positively he carried others with him. I protested that in my letter to the Board of Governors."

"You can't win, Eve."

Eve met his eyes, thinking there was much of Ken in the man's eyes.

"Not on this issue, not on the land issue," Mr. Elston said gravely. "This has now become a bitter personal quarrel between Lois and you. I happened to attend the Presentation Ball. Lois was dressed beautifully for the event. She entered the ballroom with glowing eyes and a radiant face. And saw what? Two hundred empty tables, an orchestra playing for one dancing couple, and only three of the seven governors on hand to give her the trophy. She went ashen, Eve. If ever I saw sickness come into a girl's eyes, I saw it then. But she's a Hill, all right, to her bones. She recovered beautifully. She danced with me, with each of the governors present. She accepted the trophy and she delivered her prepared speech. She left on the arm of Doug Chalmers, her head high, her back ramrod straight. And as of that moment, Eve, you had a mortal enemy. I don't exaggerate, believe me. This was her moment of glory, and you ruined it for her, deliberately or otherwise."

It left Eve with a bitter taste in her mouth. For a moment she almost wished that she'd attended the darned ball. She could have gone there with Cliff Hawkins had the others remained stubborn. And yet—

"I'll survive her enmity," she said calmly. "And actually, sir, I'll survive the loss of my land, if I must, even as I've survived the loss of the race. My father taught me to do my best and leave the rest up to God. It's a good philosophy, really."

"The Town Council condemns the land next week, Eve. Doug Chalmers has advised it, and Supervisor Wilcox has accepted the advice."

Eve nodded.

"I can still get three thousand per acre," Mr. Elston said. "But once the condemnation proceedings are instituted, the offer must be withdrawn."

"I understand, sir."

"May I point out, Eve, that fighting a thing like this can be an expensive business? The town has all the advantage. The town retains a lawyer, for instance, who is paid whether he works or doesn't work."

"I understand, sir."

"Now no one wants to be unfair, Eve. I know you have a low opinion of Supervisor Wilcox, but the fact is that it's his job to do his best for the town. He'd like to settle this thing in an amicable fashion, and in a manner fair to all. For instance, no attempt will be made to seize this fenced portion of your property, to evict you from your home. Furthermore—"

Mr. Elston never got any further. Once again a white convertible Cadillac drove up, and once again the handsome Doug Chalmers came through the gate of the white picket fence. Mr. Elston sighed and left, and after the man had driven off, Doug Chalmers took the vacated wicker chair and wagged his head. "All the world beats a path to your door, eh, Miss Barkwell? To be expected, I dare say. You're an astonishing person, actually. You have beauty, yet behave as if unaware of that. You duel with tigresses, yet seem unafraid of the fangs and claws."

"Nothing to fear, really, Mr. Chalmers. The Hills are just folks, after all."

"I imagine Mr. Elston has informed you of certain decisions that have been made?"

"He has."

"You might be wise to accept the cash offer."

"Are you concerned about my welfare?" Eve mocked. "I'm deeply touched."

He flushed. "Oh, it's possible to be ambitious, even greedy, and yet be concerned about the welfare of others."

"You're ambitious for what, Mr. Chalmers?"

He laughed. "The usual ambition for power, for a fat salary. Why not?"

"How are the prospects?"

He met her amused brown eyes. "Well, rather good," he confided. "The Hill Ethical Drugs Company is a rather dynamic outfit, Miss Barkwell. There's always opportunity if you work for an expanding, progressive organization. I rather doubt I'll ever be president of the company, but I think I might achieve a vice presidency before I'm retired."

Eve had to be impressed. "People like you awe me," she told him candidly. "You don't appear different from anyone else, and yet you're considerably different. For instance, I have to use every last bit of mental energy to keep my little Clepsydra solvent. Yet people such as yourself can cope with all the problems of a huge organization."

"It's a knack," he said casually. "You're born with it or you're not. You deserve no credit if you do have the knack, because it's something you've been given, not something you've acquired on your own. But to return to the matter of your land. While Miss Hill may not love you at the moment, she really has no desire to harm you financially. I'm told to inform you her offer remains good until the matter is referred to a court."

"Nice of her," Eve said pleasantly. "Still, it doesn't matter. I may lose this battle, too, on a technicality, but I wasn't raised to be a quitter, Mr. Chalmers."

"The difference between success and failure is

often a mere technicality, Miss Barkwell. You sail quite proficiently, by the way. If it's any satisfaction to you, you've at last convinced Lois Hill she won't ever defeat you in a scrappy-cat race."

Eve swung her gaze left at the smooth purple of Town Creek. In close to the shore, a bittern was studying a clump of reeds. The bird was so beautifully camouflaged that Doug Chalmers never did see it, not even after she had pointed out its exact location. Presently, when he'd tired of trying to spot the darned creature, Eve met his keen eyes and asked: "Are you going to marry Lois Hill, Mr. Chalmers? I've heard the rumors, of course."

"Probably. Of course you never know with Lois. In many ways, Lois is as variable as April. I never know from one month to the next, really, whether I'm in favor or out of favor. Dr. Cliff Hawkins interests her from time to time. And there are others, quite naturally."

"The reason I asked, Mr. Chalmers, is that someone ought to do something about her. The race is one thing. Pulling off my wings, so to speak, just for fun, would be something else. I would have to fight her in every way possible. The results might not be pleasant."

His head snapped back. He began to chuckle, but then he perceived in her eyes a quality that warned him this was no laughing matter.

"I'll give her your message," he said dryly. "I doubt she'll be frightened, but I'll give it to her."

"Fine," Eve said. "Now let me reward you with a message, Mr. Chalmers. Only stupid men marry to achieve the vice presidency of a corporation."

Chapter 12

At the Town Council meeting on June the twenty-eighth, Supervisor Wilcox delivered himself of a tightly knit speech. He announced that the Council was unanimous in its belief that Sather had to develop or die. He pointed out that every consultant approached by the Council had stated bluntly that the town was doing less than fifty percent of the tourist business it ought to be doing. He pointed out, also, that Creedsville farther up the river was now making a serious effort to become the vacation capital of the Eastern Shore. By next year, he announced, Creedsville would boast two marinas and a fine harbor for schooners and lesser craft. Already a large hotel was under construction. Already plans were being made to develop a recreation park for those who preferred other activities to sailing. So, Supervisor Wilcox announced, it was the opinion of the Town Council that strong efforts had to be made at once to insure Sather wouldn't become just another sleepy, half-forgotten tidewater town. The Council had therefore instructed its lawyer to take whatever legal steps were necessary to acquire the Barkwell land by means of eminent domain procedures.

For a moment, all was deep silence. Then Dorothy Holloway stood up and cried: "For shame, sir." About half a dozen fellows cheered her statement. Significantly, however, most of the older people sat there quietly, clearly troubled by the news concerning Creedsville.

Eve stood up and asked if her land were being seized for recreational purposes. Supervisor Wilcox said testily that she had heard his speech and that he'd not repeat it. Eve said this was evasion. She said she wanted a clear statement, a pledge, really, that the land would be used only for recreational purposes. If the town really wanted it for recreational purposes, she announced, she would be happy to sell it to the town for a thousand dollars an acre.

Everyone was dumbfounded, Supervisor Wilcox most of all. He stood there gaping, growing redder and redder with every passing second. Eve just stood there waiting, a fetching sight in yellow, her lustrous hair reflecting the gleams of the overhead lights. When she sensed the restlessness of the audience, she asked crisply: "Come, now, Mr. Wilcox; all you have to do is to pledge the land will be used for recreational purposes only. Yes or no?"

It happened rather as she'd thought it would. Mr. Wilcox yelled, "I don't have to give you any pledges, Miss Barkwell. The town wants that land and it'll get that land to use as it wishes."

"In other words, sir, you really want the land for commercial purposes? I doubt you can steal it from me for resale to Mr. Hill, sir. But we'll allow the court to decide that, won't we?"

Suddenly everyone was yelling that the Town

Council had to pledge the land would be used only for recreational purposes. Even the older people leaped to their feet, aware at last that there was infinitely more here than met the eye. Supervisor Wilcox lost control. He got so hopping mad with everyone that he banged his gavel and peremptorily announced that the meeting was over. Eve got the definite feeling he'd have loved to bang her head with that gavel.

On the following morning she typed a letter to the Town Council and took it up the street to have it notarized by Miss Blakewell. The chunky Miss Blakewell grinned broadly and asked: "Come to buy property, dear? Let me sell you some property. Take that building your shop is in. How clever it would be if you bought it."

"Right now I'm afraid I have too much property, Miss Blakewell. Will you notarize this, please?"

Miss Blakewell put on her thick-lensed eyeglasses and read the letter carefully. Her brows arched. Finally she looked up and announced: "Ridiculous. The fair recreational value of that land is certainly three thousand an acre. I would offer it to the Town Council at that figure, if I were you. How could the court grant you the proper compensation if you offered it, as you do here, for a thousand per acre?"

"It's my home town, you know. Wonderful folks in my home town, ma'am. For instance, no one ever told a girl, as they could have, that her father was a drunk. The women used to come to teach me to cook, keep house, all that. And the fellows! Ma'am, I'm the girl who had about two hundred brothers. The way they looked after Dad and me sometimes—well, there you are. If the town needs the land for recreational purposes, that's the price. If they can't meet the price, I'll give a mortgage at one percent for the balance."

"You don't owe anyone anything!"

Still, she notarized the letter and took it to Town Hall to make certain it reached Supervisor Wilcox personally.

A few days later Doug Chalmers dropped in, and by so doing confirmed Eve's conviction the land was wanted by the Hills for commercial purposes. The big fellow was all smiles, quite as if he'd forgiven the insinuation he was attempting to marry into a corporation vice presidency. "Care to work for Hill?" he asked. "One of my lesser chores is finding likely talent for the organization. You show promise, Miss Barkwell. Mr. Wilcox still froths at the mouth whenever your name is mentioned."

Eve led him into her small office. She waved him to the lounge chair and poured him a cup of coffee. "It seems I have a bad habit of making everyone froth at the mouth," she told him impenitently. "But just to keep the record straight, Mr. Chalmers, that message I gave you the other evening was well-meant. You'd be surprised if you knew how many in town think Lois is trying to buy you. No matter. Comes the blow?"

"Interesting development, Miss Barkwell. Did you know this building is for sale?"

"Miss Blakewell told me."

"Lois decided it would be a good investment. The arrangements were concluded just a few minutes ago. It would seem she's now your landlady."

"Fine."

"It becomes more interesting, Miss Barkwell.
Your lease expires in November."

"I have the option of renewing it."

"Provided, of course, the building is still available for commercial purposes. But Lois is far from
convinced it will be available for commercial purposes."

It jolted Eve, all right. She knew better, however, than to let him know how badly it had
jolted her.

"That's up to her, of course," she said easily.
"If I must, I can always erect a building on one of
my Town Creek acres."

"Costs money to do that."

"Well, the land isn't bringing in any money
right now, anyway."

"And then, of course, there is the little matter
of the town's determination to condemn that land.
Once you've received official notice, you'll of
course be unable to do anything with the land."

"I won't receive official notice, Mr. Chalmers.
Really, Mr. Hill is an odd man! I suppose he has

more millions than he can shake a stick at. But instead of offering me a proper price for the land, he seeks to steal it with the connivance of Mr. Wilcox. Well, it can't be done. To get that land, the town will have to prove in court it will be used for the benefit of the general public and that it's the only land in town that can be used for the stated purpose. See how much homework I've done? Well, if it will be used for recreational purposes, the town may have the land with my blessings. But it can't be snatched for resale to Mr. Hill."

"In the meantime, what do you do about this shop?"

"Do you represent Miss Hill?"

"Yes."

"I here and now inform you, Mr. Chalmers, that I won't renew the lease in November. I dislike doing business with spoiled children. Will you tell Miss Hill so?"

Doug Chalmers was flabbergasted. "Do you realize how much that decision will cost you? By the time you relocate you'll be in the hole by at least two thousand."

"My concern, isn't it?" Eve asked lightly. "Now run along, you business genuis, you. I have a living to earn at my bench."

She was actually working away quite calmly at her bench when Doug Chalmers left five minutes later. Doug Chalmers was rocked. Driving back to the Hill estate, he wondered if the lovely girl were insane or just a reckless gambler. Neither, he finally decided. It was the old case of ignorance making a person cocky. After all, why should anyone in Sather know that the old boy had squashed company after company en route to the top of the pile? The Jared Hill that folks saw in Sather was quite different from the juggernaut up north.

Doug felt sorry for the girl. Nice kid, obviously, even though she'd had it rough as a teenager. Everyone liked her. Everyone admired her, even Lois, come to think of it. She deserved a better break. After all, what did money matter to Jared Hill?

Doug kept his pity to himself, however, when he reported the results of his conversation to the

Hills in their Grecian court. He said crisply to the father and daughter: "Building acquired, the threat made, and Miss Barkwell won't renew her lease." He paused to observe the effect. Lois gasped. Mr. Hill merely continued to scratch an itch on his left ear.

"Actually," Doug continued, "I think all this is a waste of time. Miss Barkwell made a good point. The town can acquire the land through eminent domain proceedings only if it's to be used for public purposes and only if it's the best availabe land for those purposes."

Jared Hill said quietly: "Doug, I never pay a man to tell me something can't be done or that I'm wasting my time. What I want to hear from you is a course of action that will lead to success in this venture."

"Why not shoot her, sir?"

Mr. Hill looked up, frowning.

Doug sat down and crossed his legs and waited. When he thought sufficient time had elapsed, he went on: "I'd like to be general manager here, of course, sir. But if I'm to earn the post by pulling rabbits from a hat, I'm afraid I'm the wrong man. I'm no magician. I will grant that I pulled a rabbit from a hat on Race Day, but that was a fluke."

Lois looked at him sharply. "If she hadn't fouled," Lois said, "I'd have caught her and passed her."

Doug ignored her, suddenly aware that his future with the company was at that moment being decided by Mr. Jared Hill.

"Your approach is preposterous," Doug told him, risking all. "You must be worth fifty millions, sir. The land in question would cost a mere seventy-five thousand. The cost wouldn't even come out of your pocket. So why all this tomfoolery, your coronary condition considered?"

Mr. Hill asked quietly: "Have you received a better offer, Doug? Sounds as if you had."

"No, sir."

"Then why offend me?"

"I thought I was paid, sir, to handle certain business problems for you. No offense intended. The fact is that if I'd originated this approach, you yourself would call it preposterous."

Lois said heatedly: "This happened to be my idea, Doug Chalmers! For your information, I'm sick and tired of being humiliated by Eve Barkwell. I gave her a good offer. She tried to make a fool of me before the Town Council, and she tried to humiliate me on Race Day. Now it's my turn to give her a bad time, and I intend to do that."

"Kid stuff, Lois."

She sprang to her feet, lovely in her green bathing suit, her young body aquiver, but quite dangerous in her anger, too. "If you can't get the land for me," she snapped, "I know others who can."

"Call them in," Doug challenged. "Now look here, Lois. I'm sick and tired of having your father and a lot of other people think I owe my rise in the company to you. I happen to have ability. I happen to think I ought to be allowed to use that ability on something more important than aiding and abetting your vendetta against an obviously decent girl whose only real crime is that she's ten times the sailor you'll ever be. I recommend you pay her a fair price for the land. You'll never connive it from her possession and you'll never bluff it from her possession. Good heavens, be intelligent! She's older than you; she has more experience than you. All you have going for you is money, and it'll cost you more money to steal that land than it would cost to buy it."

"You shut up!"

Doug stared. He had the sick feeling suddenly that if he took that, he'd lost everything he'd worked for . . . his career with the company . . . his one opportunity to retain a reasonable self-respect. He caught Jared Hill watching him as a voracious eagle might watch the wrigglings of a helpless prey. The man's almost contemptuous eyes stung Doug. He got up and walked purposefully to Lois Hill. "Say that again," he ordered.

"I told you to shut up."

"Now apologize."

"*What?*"

"Apologize, Lois."

She began to ripple with genuine laughter, but

she stopped laughing and began to scream when Doug picked her up and tossed her into the pool.

Doug looked briefly at Jared Hill. "Either send her to her mother or teach her proper manners yourself, sir. In this day and age, fellows aren't too reluctant to paddle such as your daughter."

Lois came screeching and charging from the pool. Doug balled the fingers of his right hand into a fist and just waited. Lois stopped short, clearly rattled for a pleasant change.

"Am I fired?" Doug asked Jared Hill.

"Of course."

"Still," Doug said, "no spoiled brat tells me to shut up. Love and kisses, Lois."

Feeling quite proud of himself, all in all, Doug left.

Chapter 13

Ah, but it was a game, and a clever game at that! So Dr. Cliff Hawkins assured Eve Barkwell in early July, and he was quite content with his own view of the Hill-Chalmers breakup. Down for two weeks, for a vacation, no less, the lean, flamboyant surgeon elected himself an army of one to rout all foes of the Clepsydra. Eve discomfited him for a moment by asking directly: "Why?"

"Never do that," he ordered. "My dear girl, my dull shopkeeper, if it pleases me to aid you that is no concern of yours. From time to time one does these things, if only to retain humility. To business! Have you officially been informed of the town's fell purpose?"

Eve got the letter from the safe. The redhead at once took it off to the Sather Inn, vowing to study it closely.

Billy Taylor put his tweezers down and looked at the receding figure until Dr. Hawkins had rounded a corner. "Is he nuts, Miss Eve?" Billy asked. "A lot of folks think so, including Sally. Sally met him near Dr. Hale's building the last time he was down. You know what Dr. Hawkins did? He chucked Sally under the chin and said right out loud: 'My, there's a pretty!' A good thing Sally was raised right. She wanted to kick him on the shin."

"The compliment was probably sincere. That's a quality in Dr. Hawkins that impresses me. His sincerity, I mean. Tell your Sally to humor him."

Bill returned to work. His assignment this humid afternoon was a Seth Thomas eight-day clock that required a new bushing as well as a thorough cleaning. Eve had decided to put him onto clocks almost exclusively for the next two months, her thought being that at the end of that time she could turn over most clock jobs to him. A raise would go with his assignment to real responsibility, but she'd deliberately not told Bill that, knowing that he'd work too darned tensely to demonstrate he was worth the extra money.

Eve watched him for a time, delighting in the deftness with which he disassembled the clock. While she was still far from convinced she was the best teacher any apprentice could have, there was little doubt in her mind now that her painstaking training of Billy had brought him along nicely. Whatever he knew, he knew thoroughly; moreover, he was more enthusiastic about the trade today than he'd been even the morning she'd offered him a job. One day, she thought contentedly, Billy would prosper nicely in a shop of his own. He might even marry his Sally. Think of that! Think of actually having played a small role in the development of a human being!

The talk involving Doug Chalmers had left her too disturbed, though, just to stand there doing nothing. It seemed to her that if Doug Chalmers had gone to bat for her, as Dr. Cliff

Hawkins had claimed, then she certainly ought to reciprocate as best she could. Why not confront the eagle? Wasn't it about time someone did? Who was Lois Hill, after all, without the man who had earned the millions that had made her so powerful? And why in the world should anyone assume that Mr. Jared Hill entirely approved everything his daughter did?

Eve headed for the Hill estate, just ambling along to give herself a chance to think over the things she wanted to say. Near the bank, however, she met Ken, and Ken pretended to be aghast. "You'd better learn to drive," Ken told her. "Don't you know that walking on a humid day like this can kill you? Where to?"

"Just ambling around. Is your father still involved in the land grab?"

Ken's jaws tightened. "No. He agreed there's something odd in Wilcox's refusal to pledge the land will be used for recreation and recreational facilities. So after a long discussion, he terminated his involvement in the matter."

"Good. The fact is, Ken, that we'll need a new

supervisor next year. I've tried to give Mr. Wilcox the benefit of every doubt, but it's apparent he's no longer as impartial as a town supervisor ought to be. Frankly, I think Mr. Hill wants the land for commercial purposes, and I also think Mr. Wilcox expects to get something for himself by serving the Hill interests."

"I understand your lease won't be renewed."

"Quite correct. Does the bank know of a nice little building that could be moved onto my property? It wouldn't have to be a large building. Say one of those little real-estate office buildings they put up when they want to sell tract houses right in the tract."

"I'll look into it."

Ken glanced at his watch, and Eve took the hint and ambled on. When she reached the Hill estate she was careful to do everything properly. Instead of just barging in between the stone gate posts, she pressed the bell button of the care-taker's cottage and sat waiting patiently on the doorstep until Mr. Cluett came hustling along. Mr. Cluett rolled his eyes when he saw her. "Miss

Eve," he remonstrated, "you got better sense. Go 'long now! Ain't you wanna live?"

"Hi, Mr. Cluett. How's Aunt Mary?"

"You wanna see Mr. Jared Hill or Miss Lois Hill?" he asked. "Don't say I didn't warn you, though."

"Mr. Hill, please."

Mr. Cluett went into the fieldstone cottage and apparently telephoned the main house. Presently he drove Eve along the blue gravel road to the huge white frame. "I'll wait right here," he said. "Ain't nothin' I can do for you inside, Miss Eve, but I can sure drive you away in a hurry."

"Oh, they're civilized people, Mr. Cluett. I'll be quite all right."

Aunt Mary gave her the ghost of a smile at the door but said not a word. She led Eve to a small, comfortable sitting room on the second floor. Mr. Hill was alone there, listening to a play-by-play baseball broadcast involving the Colts and the Yankees. He switched off the radio when she entered, and he rose. "A pleasant surprise," he said softly. "It troubles me, Miss Barkwell, that not once this year have I dropped in to enjoy your clock collection. Several of your clocks fascinate me."

"You're always welcome, sir. Did Dr. Cliff Hawkins tell you of his passion for the Fifi? He was quite vexed when I told him it isn't for sale."

"An odd young man. Occasionally I wonder if perhaps I ought not have a different doctor. Yet Dick Hale assures me he's good. It's an odd thing about ability, Miss Barkwell. Ability is often packaged most unimpressively. And then, at other times, as in your case, it is packaged beautifully."

Eve inclined her head prettily, and a faint smile quirked his lips. Yet, the smile notwithstanding, the thin, cold face remained thin and cold.

"Your business?" he asked. "But perhaps I ought to say first that I will not interfere in any way in this conflict between Lois and you. To be honest, Miss Barkwell, it rather delights me to see my girl displaying her present interest in business matters."

"Oh, I can handle Lois, sir. Nothing your daughter can say or do will bother me very much.

I simply wanted to know if all this commotion about the land is really necessary. It's for sale if my price is met. If the town wants it for the people, the price is a thousand an acre. If you want it for commercial purposes, the price is fifteen thousand an acre."

"Why should I want it for commercial purposes, Miss Barkwell?"

"Perhaps you don't. But if you don't, sir, then your daughter's attitude is odd. Why should she want to pay three thousand an acre for land I'll sell at a thousand an acre if it will be used as Mr. Wilcox claims but won't guarantee it will be used?"

"Allow me to ask *you* a question, Miss Barkwell. Why are you so intent upon depriving my daughter of the good will she would win if she presented that land to the town?"

"That hasn't ever been my intention, sir. I think Lois tends to exaggerate her difficulties with me. I've never been an enemy or even a rival. To me, Lois was just another contestant in each of the races we both entered. I trained for all of them, not to defeat Lois specifically but to defeat as many as I could; to win, in short. Apart from the inevitable competition there, I've never competed against her in anything else. And I'm not trying to do anything in this case except insure I won't be hoodwinked out of the price I ought to receive for the land if it's used commercially."

"Well, as I've said, I will not interfere. It will surprise me greatly if Lois fails to give you trouble. What did you expect? Only an idiot grabs a tiger by the tail."

Eve decided she might as well give *him* food for thought. "I fight tigers with tigers, sir," she told him. "I understand Mr. Doug Chalmers is now unemployed. So I've decided to let him do my fighting with your daughter. Interesting?"

His reaction was certainly interesting. The faint smile he'd worn throughout their discussion became a broad and quite warm grin of admiration. "I begin to think," he said, "that you are wasting your time in the Clepsydra, Miss Barkwell. Very shrewd stroke! Have you ever considered broadening your scope? My company is a rather dynamic organization, and certainly there's room in it for a clever person."

Eve rose, chuckling. "I'm afraid I'm much too contented with my lot, Mr. Hill. I love repairing watches. I love having my own shop, my own cottage, my own life. Perhaps I'd make more money if I were more ambitious, but I doubt I'd be happier."

"How is your father?"

"Grand, sir. He's now worked a full month, and he tells me he rather enjoys it."

"Good. You understand, don't you, there's nothing personal behind any business battle the Hills might wage? I mean, Miss Barkwell, that I would always aid you and your father in a non-business way if that became necessary. We're human beings, after all."

Eve thought, after she'd left: no wonder poor Lois was so strange!

Chapter 14

Predictably, Doug Chalmers came to the cottage to ask a bit angrily just when he had agreed to relieve Eve of the necessity to battle Sather for her land. For the occasion, Eve was wearing a flowered print. Every curl was in place, and even her fingernails had been seen to. She received Mr. Doug Chalmers in her living room, a fact that rather surprised him. "What about your reputation?" he asked. "People in tank towns have antique notions about how a girl ought to behave."

"Fine reputation," Eve assured him. "But if it will make you any happier, we'll do all our kissing outdoors. All right?"

He chuckled and sat down. He gazed about the

room with interest. The paneling interested him particularly. "What sort of wood?" he asked.

"Redwood. My father paneled this room without help, too. I suppose a professional carpenter would notice some goofs, particularly the faulty mitering of the moldings. Pop was always proud of the job he did, though, and so am I."

The homey appearance of the room tended to smooth his ruffled feathers. Slowly, with evident pleasure, he looked at each piece of maple furniture, at the green and red braided rug, at the old-brick fireplace. "You do very well for yourself," he commented. "I earn sixteen thousand a year but don't live nearly as well as this."

"Perhaps, then, you ought to analyze your so-called success. The only reason for earning money is to provide yourself and your loved ones the most agreeable life possible. A very wise man told me that once—a banker from Wilmington, Delaware. He used to come to my porch often. He liked to sit there and watch the water and listen to the birds. He was a quite unhappy man, poor dear. He had worked terribly hard all his life to amass a fortune. His wife died, his daughter married a man he disapproved of, and there the old fellow was, possessed of a fortune and utterly miserable with it. Yet he couldn't sell his great town house and come here to live in a cottage such as this. It would be stepping down, he said. Imagine! Do you know how I answered him? Sir, I told him, it's but a skip and a jump from the cradle to the grave. Life is much too short, I told him, for anyone to concern himself even for a moment with anything but the happiness of himself and others."

"Yet there can be happiness in accomplishment, Miss Barkwell."

"Oh, call me Eve. Everyone calls me Eve. No tar on my reputation if you call me Eve, I assure you. Accomplishment, now! Mr. Doug Chalmers, for shame! I'll concede that Lois Hill is essentially a fine girl, but what accomplishment is there in taking advantage of her innocence and loneliness to climb to the position you've reached?"

"Now wait a moment!"

"No, sir. This may astonish you, but I do have

a certain fondness for Lois. Lois is still regularly sending some money for Billy's salary every week. There's a fine person! And you're fine, too. I have news for you, Mr. Chalmers. I was deeply touched when I learned you'd incurred the mighty Hill wrath by calling me an obviously decent girl whose only real crime is that I'm ten times the sailor Lois will ever be."

Doug gaped.

"Lois was probably less touched," Eve commented dryly. "I think that's why she told you to shut up. Rude of her. Self-indulgent people are often rude."

"Who told you all this?" Doug asked.

"Mr. Cluett and Aunt Mary. The Cluetts are good friends of mine, Doug."

"They could be fired for telling tales out of school. How do you know you haven't just cost them their jobs?"

"Isn't your future the more important question?"

Reminded, he grimaced. "Now look," he said, "I never agreed to handle your land battle for you. I resent the fib you told Mr. Hill. Lois is fit to be tied. She came to the inn last night and made a row. I'm to return to Philadelphia at once."

"Really?"

Her mocking eyes discomfited Doug Chalmers. It seemed to him he knew exactly what she was thinking, and it troubled him to know she was right. Still, what else could he do? It was a rough world. Ability alone didn't carry you far, because others were as able. You needed something more, an edge, the sort of edge he'd acquired the day Lois Hill had discovered he appealed to her.

"Isn't it a big price to pay for success?" Eve asked gently. "I think it is. Perhaps I'm silly, but I do believe marriage ought to mean more than that. What are you afraid of, Doug? That you can't manage without the Hills? Well, I manage without them and even despite them."

He asked testily: "Do you think I'm unaware of that? And I'm impressed by you, believe me. You could have let her out-sail you on Race Day; you could have let her have the land. And by doing all that, you could have gained a lot, Lois being that way, and you knew it. Still, you sailed to win and you're scrapping here to win. Cheers. Only you have your own business, and I don't. Only you're not within shooting distance of a big income, and I am. Do you know what the general manager of a Hill research plant earns? Twenty-five thousand dollars a year."

Eve saw it, then, and was startled. "And he wants my acreage for the plant, isn't that so?"

Doug scowled, looking down at his shoes.

"You don't work for him now," Eve pointed out. "You work for me, if you wish, but not for them."

"If I followed orders and returned to Philadelphia I'd still be on the payroll."

"With a glittering future ahead of you, Doug? I think not. You see, you blundered. You should never have minimized her sailing ability. I'm sure that at the time the foul was claimed, Lois was convinced she could have caught me had I followed the mapped course. Lois has reasonable honesty, you know, and she's reasonably fair. I don't think she'd have called the foul had—"

"Still, I'm going to Philadelphia."

"You'll be fired within three months, Doug. Lois won't do it because she won't have to. You were given an assignment, and you never made a serious effort to carry it out. Mr. Hill respects me because I'm competent in my trade. I don't think he respects anyone who fails. So Lois won't see you, and the word will get around, and then what?"

He drew a deep breath. "I won't cheat my way to the top," he said grimly. "The plan here was downright dishonest. They thought you'd grab the first offer that was made, which is why they handled it as they did. Then Lois got into the act, thinking to make a big name for herself as a benefactress of the town. But her offer was too high. You became suspicious, and the fat was in the fire. Now Lois has to get that land or accept the fact you have the edge on her, money notwithstanding. I was supposed to organize a boycott of your shop, force you out of the building. You were then supposed to open a shop here on your property. The idea was to wait until you did, then have the Town Council close you down for conducting a business in an area zoned for residential purposes only. Well, for Pete's sake, you're a decent girl. I wouldn't do a thing like that to any girl."

Eve could have kissed him, she was so pleased with him. Instead, she did what appeared to her to be the next best thing for him, for herself, for Sather. She sat down at her maple desk and got a sheet of notepaper from the drawer. She wrote quickly, signed her name with a flourish and blotted the ink dry. She gave him the paper without a word and then went outdoors to her porch. She had to sit down hurriedly, for it occurred to her suddenly that this was the first fellow she had ever trusted with something quite precious to her. She wondered, baffled, why she'd done so. Sure, the fellow was handsome and she loved the way he backed up his principles with action. But she'd met handsomer men, men of principle—Rod and Ken and Dr. Cliff Hawkins, for example.

Glory, she wondered, was the strain of this ridiculous cat fight impairing her judgment?

The door opened. Under Doug's weight, the

tongue-and-groove porch floorboards creaked. He came to her chair and stood behind her and asked: "Do you know what you've done, Eve? You've given me a great success. If Mr. Hill respects competence, then he'll certainly respect me when I sell him the land, no strings attached, for a thousand an acre. Listen, lady, are you crazy? You don't hand a fellow you don't know a scrap of paper appointing him sole agent to make whatever deal he thinks best for your five acres."

"But I'm just a small town watchmaker, you see, a person who must use her judgment for better or worse because she can't afford to hire a staff of experts to help her. Is the twenty-five per cent commission adequate?"

"You're trying to reform me, aren't you?"

"Returning kindness for kindness, I think."

"You've never been as poor as I, Eve. Had you been, you'd have known this is silly."

But ah, the wistfulness in his rich voice!

"You remind me of Billy Taylor," Eve told him. "Billy wanted to be a watchmaker but lacked the nerve to approach me for a job. You want to be less of a vulture, say, but lack the nerve to try to be your own man."

"Vulture?"

"Picking money, power, greatness from the childish crush of a great man's daughter! A very vulturish thing, it seems to me."

He came around the chair, flushed, eyes flashing. Eve grinned up at him, quite unafraid. Her big brown eyes fascinated him, and it occurred to him quite sharply that here was a quite attractive young woman. He looked down at the commission she'd given him. "Want this back?"

"No."

"Last chance."

"So be it."

"But you can't trust me!"

"Now I'd like to go for a ride," Eve told him simply. "I've never ridden in an elegant Cadillac."

"Pfui!"

He stalked off and gunned the car from the gate. Eve chuckled, finding his behavior rather boyish, but cute, too. In a happy frame of mind, feeling that now, at last, she could forget the land question and concentrate upon her own emotional affairs, she went back into the cottage and telephoned Dr. Cliff Hawkins at Sather Inn.

"Dear one," he begged, "never interrupt a man at his thinking, there's a sweet."

"I wondered if it's possible, Cliff, that a man of your experience has perceived the eternal gold under the silly facade called Lois Hill."

A long, long silence.

"Your interest in me has been touching, of course," Eve assured him, "and I'll never forget it, Cliff. But unless one is terribly conceited, one doubts the sincerity of quickly won adoration, particularly when one has had the opportunity to study the reactions of the fellow to Lois Hill."

"Now, now . . ."

"Cliff, would it be a foolish girl, do you think, who dated a jobless cross between a vulture and a nice guy?"

"Doug?"

With this man, Eve could be herself. "Dreadful though it may sound," she said crisply, "he interests me."

Chapter 15

Lois Hill continued to believe it was all merely a matter of time. Despite the warnings of Dr. Cliff Hawkins, she sat tight on the land question and made absolutely no effort to bring Doug Chalmers to heel. Lois was quite convinced any court in the county would uphold the Town Council's right to seize land for worth-while public purpose. She was also quite convinced that as soon as Doug had lost a few paychecks he would come to her with his hat in his hand. Lois looked forward with particular relish to this latter event. Humiliate her, would he, before her own father? Well, now!

August, therefore, was a pleasant month for

Lois Hill. She spent many hours sailing, and had the satisfaction of scoring many victories in impromptu races with other craft encountered on the river. Evenings were quite agreeable, too, for Dr. Cliff Hawkins decided to give himself a real vacation and came to take her out six nights out of seven. He was outlandishly florid in his compliments, and sometimes these and his rather quaint gallantries moved her to fits of delighted laughter. But best of all, Cliff was not a fellow to scold her, to reform her, to improve her. He seemed to like her exactly as she was, whether she kicked off her slippers at formal parties or drove at ninety miles an hour in a thirty-mile zone. And the things he could tell a girl when they were alone in the *Victory* on a moonlit sea!

But toward the end of August a rather disturbing thing happened. One of the county judges unofficially informed Supervisor Wilcox that the eminent domain proceedings instituted by the town would have no chance whatever of being upheld unless and until the documents submitted stated the specific reason the land in question was urgently needed. Supervisor Wilcox argued heatedly that sometimes it was necessary to leave things vague so that people couldn't profit from an announced piece of action. The argument was dismissed out of hand. "It is generally known," the judge said, "that you wish to create a recreation area there. Inasmuch as the news is out, you won't be hurt by stating your reasons for seeking this land."

Somehow, the news was leaked to elderly Miss Elias. The *Sather Record* headlined the unofficial decision. Then a worse thing happened. Doug Chalmers, of all people, issued a statement that the unofficial decision was the best blow struck for justice in the history of the county. He went on to state it was really common knowledge that the Hills were trying to grab the land for commercial purposes and that Supervisor Wilcox was only a tool the Hills were using.

Cliff said lugubriously: "I told you so, sweet. Inevitable, really. They sail daily, this man and Eve Barkwell. Is he smitten? Is she smitten? My opinion is that they are. Pack him up, send him home, and make your peace with Eve Barkwell forthwith."

Still, Lois just couldn't believe it. It came to her that Doug was playing the old game of trying to make so much trouble for the Hills that the Hills would buy him off. Lois curled her lip contemptuously. "Without me he was nothing," she cried hotly, "and without me he's still nothing!"

But now she began to notice that practically every day, usually in late afternoon or early evening, she saw the *Vixen* on the water, Doug at the helm, Eve sitting on a gunwale. And they always seemed to be having such a good time! Paupers! Stupid! Yet there they were, having a good time, quite as if they had nothing to fear.

Furious, Lois asked her father to bring some topnotch lawyers down to Sather. He obliged. The lawyers heard her out, examined the documents. Reilly then said: "Absolutely impossible, Miss Hill. If I were representing the other side, I would challenge the town on its motives. I would compel the town to state those motives, and I would then ask the court to draw up an order allowing the seizure for only the stated purpose."

"I know that, Mr. Reilly. What I don't know is how we get around that."

"Neither do I."

"Preposterous! There's always an out; ask Daddy."

"Not in this case, Miss Hill, because, apparently, Miss Barkwell is willing that her land be used for recreational purposes. The only time there's an out is if the other party is really striving to make a deal. In this case, obviously . . ."

"You're fired!"

Mr. Reilly chuckled. "But I don't work for you, Miss Hill. Your father is a friend. I came down with my assistants merely to oblige him."

And hard on that came the second blow.

In the name of Eve Barkwell, Doug Chalmers rose at a Town Council meeting in mid-September and requested permission of the Council for Eve Barkwell to establish a small shop on the property immediately adjacent to her pier. Mr. Wilcox ruled crisply that permission was denied on the grounds that the land was located in a residential zone. Doug Chalmers smilingly pointed out that if the town used this technicality now, it would have to use the same technicality if, say, someone acquired the land in dispute and tired to use it for business purposes.

Lois wanted to choke him.

Flushed, suddenly perspiring, Supervisor Wilcox said after a time that perhaps he ought to consult with others of the Council.

During the long wait, Lois glared at Doug, trying to will him to meet her eyes. But he never looked her way once. He sat talking with one of the inland farmers, old Mr. Goldsmith, quite as if he had not a care in the world.

The final ruling brought a patter of applause from the twenty or so townspeople in the audience. "The Town Council reverses me," Supervisor Wilcox said, "and grants Miss Barkwell permission to establish a small shop within the fenced portion of her land on Town Creek."

Lois leaped to her feet. "I protest!" she declared. "Either a zone is a residential zone or it is not."

"The fact is, Miss Hill," Supervisor Wilcox said uncomfortably, "that if we establish this land can be used only for residential purposes, then none of that land can be used for anything else."

Feeling foolish and not enjoying the sensation, Lois whirled on Doug Chalmers. "Very clever, you traitor," she snapped.

Now it became her passion to defeat him. How dare he betray her, she who had made him, she who had lifted him from the gutter? Sputtering all the way home, Lois went into urgent conference the moment she found her father.

"I want Doug, sir," she said.

"Indeed?"

"His throat."

"The doctor is now preferable?"

"Why not?"

"Just about old enough to be your father."

"It doesn't matter. Cliff understands me. He likes me as I am."

"If he does that, young lady, he loves you. I, for example, frequently dislike you as you are."

"I've always known that."

"Have you, now?"

"I'm not David, you see, a son to work into the business. And I do have this regrettable loyalty to my mother. That has always bothered you, too."

"That will be all, Lois."

"It isn't even the beginning! You got me into this, just to keep the record straight. You scolded me for what you called blabbing. I didn't know you wanted that land for a research plant. I thought Eve was being offered an unfair price, and I offered her a fair price. So you became angry, didn't you? Now here I am, and you haven't even had the decency to try to help me once."

"But I have."

"How?"

"Lois, you merely represented opportunity to Doug Chalmers. Well, Doug is out of your life, and I think it's fair to claim I helped you in that matter."

"How?"

"My dear girl, do you think for an instant I didn't know Doug had been given an impossible assignment? Do you think for an instant I ever believed your silly pressure technique would work? No. But you seemed to be having an interesting time during this, your first business battle. Moreover, Doug appeared to be having a difficult conflict with his conscience. So I sat by and awaited the inevitable failure, the inevitable success."

"Failure?"

Reilly's word is good with me. If he states the thing is legally impossible, then it is. You're wasting your time."

"But if you knew that—"

"I detest poor sports," Mr. Hill said coldly. "Do you think I was proud of you the day you called that foul? I give Doug credit for having told you the truth. You were defeated that day because you sailed ineptly from beginning to end."

"But—"

"Naturally, I was curious to learn how you would handle this small business problem. I will say this for you: you do fight with determination if not with skill.''

"For shame! Not once in my life have I ever left you out on a limb!''

"May I ask a question?''

"No.''

"Shall I reemploy Doug? I rather like his spirit, his quick eye for the weakness in a situation. Yet Doug is a reasonable man, as all good businessmen ought to be. He telephoned yesterday that he'll accept twelve thousand an acre.''

"Don't you dare!''

"Are you sure?''

His eyes were so hard that they gave Lois pause. She sat down breathlessly, beginning to understand that on this evening of defeat she was standing at a crossroads in her life.

"Where I failed with your mother,'' Mr. Jared Hill confided, "was in assuming her home and social position and children would be enough. It never for an instant occurred to me that my absorption in business would trouble her so. So the years sped by, and we drifted farther apart until nothing was left, not even anger or hatred. Is that what you want from your husband, Lois?"

"What on earth are you talking about?"

"If Doug returns, young lady, he has you under his thumb. From that moment on, all will be as he dictates. Regardless of your poor opinion of my love for you, I would make him executive vice president under David. What will that mean? A town house, all the appurtenances of success, and all the challenges and excitements of big business. I can see Doug doing as I did, becoming more and more absorbed in business. And you?"

"Stop it!"

Jared Hill nodded, having at last gotten the information he wanted. "A girl of nineteen," he said, "ought to have better sense than to leave Doug, in his present state of mind, to an attractive, warm-hearted woman such as Eve Barkwell."

"He walked out!"

"He walked out."

"He had no right to talk as he did!"

"He had no right."

"Well, then?"

Jared Hill smiled wearily. "Be adult, Lois. If

he's the fellow, then he's the fellow. Certainly it's always distasteful to seek a person out to apologize to him. It would be more distasteful, though, I'm afraid, to hear of the fellow's marriage to some other woman."

Lois drew a deep breath. "But that's ridiculous!"

"No. Doug Chalmers has come up with an interesting business idea. According to Mr. Elston at the bank, Chalmers wants to establish an agency through which all the independent farmers of this area can market their produce. The thing is interesting because the agent who controls that produce controls many needed tons of marketable items. A deal could be made with a large canner or frozen-food house on a volume basis. Doug could collect from the farmers on one hand and the selected company on the other hand."

"What does Doug know about farming?"

"According to Mr. Elston, it was Eve Barkwell's idea. That girl fascinates me, I'm afraid. Under other circumstances, she might have had a notable career."

Lois went white. She stood there, her bosom heaving, her lips ground into a thin line.

Jared Hill understood. He said gently, "I have never loved you more than at this moment, Lois. You're no quitter, I'll tell you that. You didn't quit the day of the race; you didn't quit when Doug betrayed you. For what it's worth, let me say that if I can ever play a losing hand with your spirit, I'll be quite content with myself."

"She won't have him."

"I think so."

"Daddy, that would be too much! Don't you see, this was all just a kind of game! If she'd behaved at all properly on Race Day, none of this would have happened."

"Care to go to Paris?" he asked. "It's been a trying summer for you, hasn't it?"

She gave him one withering glance and walked upstairs to her room.

There must be a way, she thought. There was always a way if you used your brains and your money. This Eve Barkwell was no supergirl.

Think!

Chapter 16

The venture moved well for Doug. On September twentieth he was able to report to Eve in her office in the Clepsydra that her introductions to Mr. Goldsmith and several other older farmers had given him all the opportunity he'd needed to sell his ideas in areas that counted. One by one he took signed documents from his briefcase and laid them on her desk. "The Tilneys, the Bensons, the Athelwhites, the Goldsmiths, the Dorans," he recited. "Also, the Harknesses, the Doolittles, the—"

"Very impressive," Eve interrupted, smiling. "You must be a talented salesman. I never did think you could talk the Tilneys into joining your group."

Doug sat down on a corner of the desk. His eyes had a luster of triumph. "Quite accidental," he confessed. "I happened to hear of an outfit in Cambridge that needs hay. The Tilneys are loaded with hay. When Tilney asked bluntly what I could do for him that he couldn't do for himself, I told him I could empty one of his hay barns that same day. He gave me a dubious look but said I could go ahead. I called the Cambridge outfit, and they came and took away all the carry-over from last year. Mr. Tilney asked what my commission was. I told him ten percent. I then pointed out it would have been just five percent had he been signed up with my group. In that case, I told him, the Cambridge outfit would have paid the other five percent. He signed up. But he did give me a check for the ten percent on the hay."

"You'll need a boat next year, Doug. A lot of stuff could be sold in Cambridge and other places if you could transport your stuff to the market."

"Nope."

"Why not?"

"A sizable boat is a big investment, and it lies idle too much of the time."

"You could make regular freight runs."

"Nope."

"Why not?"

"Take Jared Hill. A great man. He could be in a hundred other businesses as well as the drug business. But he sticks to drugs exclusively. Why? Simple. By concentrating on the manufacture and sale of drugs, he keeps abreast of all developments both product-wise and market-wise. This present business will be all I can handle efficiently for quite some time. I want to expand to other areas as soon as practicable. A lot of work in that for just one man."

"No help from Ken Elston?"

"The best help of all, Eve. The son isn't the father by a long shot. He put his own personal capital into the agency. Also, he's given nice leads from time to time. Fine. If he handles the financial and legal matters, that will be more than enough."

"He'll handle them. Ken is deceptive. A great

many people think he wouldn't be in the bank if it weren't for his father. But Ken handles most of the bank's real estate transactions, and they make money."

Up front, the bells on the entrance door jingled. It was Dr. Cliff Hawkins. The lean redhead gazed wistfully at the Fifi clock. "Dear girl," he told Eve, "I'll have a performance, pray."

"Which one!"

"I would have the ballerina, dear girl. If one may not have the name, one may as well have the illusion."

Eve worked the switch, wound the clock and pushed the minute hand close to the hour. The music box tinkled a lovely chord, and the Fifi rose to her toes atop the white circus horse. Then she twirled around so prettily that Dr. Cliff Hawkins was ravished. "I bid a thousand," he said. "A thousand for the Fifi."

The telephone rang.

Billy Taylor answered it.

His eyes bugged. "Did you say *Mr.* Barkwell, sir?"

Dr. Hawkins chuckled. "Oh, yes, dear girl, I quite forgot. The family ought to stay together. Blood is thicker than water and all that, eh? So to New York. Stern lecture to a self-doubting individual, a mere tradesman by the name of Barkwell. When is death not death? When is the hour for brooding, the hour for love? Quite a remarkable lecture, true, but then, I'm a remarkable man. My dear girl, I could have a vein from your finger before you ever missed it. Quite! At any rate—"

"Cliff, will you be *still?*"

There was stillness, save for the music box, the tinkling of an Offenbach fragment fit for a prima ballerina such as the Fifi. Now the pirouette, now the dip, now the graceful fluttering of the arms . . .

Eve said: "Of course, Pop. Of course, of course, of course. Gollygoshgee, Pop, welcome home!"

Doug Chalmers came out of the office. Cliff eyed him frigidly. "You, sir," he declared, "are an abomination."

"Hi, Cliff," Doug said easily.

"Hi, old man. Quite the intellect, aren't you?

Or are you?"

With shaking hands, with little tears in her eyes blurring the darned thing, Eve stopped the Fifi clock. She picked it from the counter and carried it straight to Dr. Cliff Hawkins. "To a very great man, with gratitude," she said simply. "Cliff, I adore you!"

"Naturally. All adore, but no one marries. Still, one has his eyes and his eternal hope, eh? A present for me? How touching!"

Eve left him there, grinning over the Fifi clock. She hit the street in full stride and never stopped running until she'd reached her cottage and the thin, graying, smiling man in the wicker chair on the front porch. "Pa," she whispered, panting, "how nice. Did you bring your tools with you? Pa, you'll just have to train Billy as you did me."

"Is he bright?"

"Of course he's bright."

"I'll train him, then. I like to train young people to be watchmakers. It's the best trade there is. To me, it's the only trade there is."

"Here; let me open the door."

He chuckled. "Now there's a funny thing, Eve. Something told me the screen on the back window near the service door still wasn't latched. And the back window still wasn't locked. So I went in that way."

Eve drew a deep breath.

Albert Barkwell said simply, "It was all right, daughter. I went to the room and I stayed there awhile and nothing happened. That fellow Hawkins knows his business. It just felt good to be there again."

"Grand."

"Do you ever think how strange life is, what it can do to people?"

"I was never much for long, long thoughts, Pop. I'm not much of a thinker, I dare say."

"Well, it doesn't matter. I had a thought there, but it doesn't matter. I can repair watches again, Eve. I was a bit rusty, of course, but the knack came back much more quickly than I thought it would. I'll be of use in the shop."

"Goop, you'll *be* the shop."

He laughed, and they went indoors. Eve carried

one of his bags into the master bedroom, then loped into the kitchen to make him the thick, too sweet cocoa he'd always loved. He came out to sit down at the table and watch her work, and while she worked, they talked.

"Still keep in touch with the nuns at the hospital, Pop?"

"Yes. And with Betsy Wrong."

"Betsy *who*?"

"A nurse I met there. She always said that no matter what she did, she did it wrong. That was true, if you looked at it as she did. But it wasn't true if you looked at it the way I did. For instance, she'd stand there for an hour letting me talk about my wife. It's queer the things you tell nurses, huh? You know about nurses, Eve? Next to watchmakers, they're the real salt of the earth. I asked Betsy Wrong to come down here for Thanksgiving."

"We'll buy a goose, a turkey and an elk!"

"Silly."

"Happy."

"Your Ma used to be happy in this kitchen.

Time after time I'd sit here like this, with your Ma making cocoa as I like it. Do you know what? I should have remembered that, Eve. According to Betsy Wrong, the thing to remember isn't what's lost but what's been had. Real profound, that, and Betsy's only twenty!"

"Add a whale to the Thanksgiving feed!"

"Silly."

The doorbell rang. Eve excused herself and hurried to answer, thinking it was Cliff and Doug come to see how the wanderer and she were making out. Almost the instant she opened the door she wanted to close it. Too late. Chic in an autumn suit, her smile bright, her gray eyes steady, young Lois Hill gestured at the family limousine and announced: "I thought I'd say goodbye, darling. Interesting summer and all that, but so much to do in dear Philadelphia and lovely Paris."

"How nice of you to drop by! Care for some oversweet cocoa? My father's come home, and we were about to indulge in the kitchen."

"No time, really. One thing more, a small thing, really, but interesting to me. May I buy him back?"

"Buy him back?"

"Doug."

"Oh?"

"The building in which the shop is located, and twelve thousand for each of your five acres."

"Are your serious?"

"Quite."

"How could I possibly sell Doug to you?"

"Turn me down, darling, and what happens to the brute? Oh, I fancy he'll earn a living; most people do, stupid though they may be. But will that satisfy Doug? I think not."

"Why not ask Doug, Lois?"

"They're so unrealistic during their little moments of infatuation, you see. But we women are different—infinitely more practical, infinitely more realistic, infinitely more—"

"Now aren't you silly?" Eve asked, exasperated. "Lois Hill, it's about time you grew up. I'm sick and tired of your nonsense! You're a wretched sailor and a wretched businesswoman and a spoiled brat who deserves to be soundly spanked.

You fool, you! Any man you can buy isn't worth having, and any trickery you can devise isn't worth devising. I don't own your Mr. Doug Chalmers or your Dr. Cliff Hawkins or anyone else. Really!"

"Naturally," Lois said, "I'll instruct my secretary to mail Billy's check, as always."

"Why?"

"Why?"

Eve sighed, remembering her father in the kitchen. "I'd be a social worker if I were you, Lois. You may not make much money, but you don't need the money and you do enjoy helping people."

"When I want your advice, I'll ask for it!"

"Have a nice autumn and winter, there's a dear."

"And next year I'll lick you on Race Day!"

Eve waited, knowing the girl too well to think that was the end of it.

Lois sighed. "Well, you may continue to rent the space in the building, and if you'll accept my price for the land, that will be that."

"Accepted."

The gray eyes of Lois Hill began to shine.

Victory!

She'd done it, she'd done it, she'd done it!

But Lois mastered her elation. Nor did she ever let Eve know that she'd have paid the full fifteen thousand for each acre.

A Hill, Lois nodded coolly. "Have your representative get in touch with my father, please. A nice autumn and winter to you, too, of course."

Eve didn't know whether to laugh or cry a little as the girl went with considerable majesty to the waiting Lincoln limousine.

Chapter 17

Ken Elston conceded it was quite a problem. He said frankly that he was unqualified to handle such a problem or even to advise anyone on how to handle it. "Show me land," Ken said ruefully, "and I can tell you what to do with it. But people baffle me. What makes them tick? What makes you tick, Eve? Here's what I mean. All the odds were in her favor. On Race Day she had the better boat. Throughout the summer she had all the advantages money could give her. Yet she walks off, the loser, and you sit here, the winner."

"Nonsense, Ken. First of all, she didn't have the better boat. For sprints, yes, but not for racing under all-weather conditions. As for the money:

no advantage there, because I had possession of the thing in contention, the land. For goodness sake, don't ever underestimate that young lady! I had the advantages, yet she did get the scrappy-cat trophy and she might have gotten the land had Doug been less of a person than he is."

"Speaking of whom, are you going to marry him, as Lois appears to believe?"

"Yes."

Spoken flatly, it was all the more jarring to a fellow who had dreamed a dream for as long as he could remember. "Eve," he remonstrated, "isn't that pretty sudden? After all, you can't know him very well."

"The event won't be sudden," she assured him. "As you say, I don't know him very well. Also, there's so much to do. Hang it, Ken, I have still another problem. This one involves Pop. Actually, it should be his shop, now that he's home. But he insists I'm the owner, the boss. How do you give orders to your own father?"

"Such as?"

"Well, he's softened. He used to drive me and

drive me. But Billy wraps Pop around his little finger. For instance, Pop just closed the shop yesterday afternoon and took Billy for a drive because Billy said he wanted to see the fall colors. I ask you!"

"Now that problem is easily handled," Ken said. "You dock both the loafers a full day's wages."

"I did."

"And?"

"They're picketing the Clepsydra. Actually! When I left, Pop was carrying a sign and Billy was making a sign. I don't know if Pop brings out the imp in Billy or Billy brings out the imp in Pop."

"Fire 'em!"

Eve's eyes flashed. "Then I'll have to support them both, you ninny!"

Ken chuckled.

Eve said thoughtfully: "Returning to the first problem, I suppose the thing to do is send Doug Chalmers to Mr. Hill. Ken, let's be honest a moment. Even if Doug does very well in this new venture, he won't earn at most more than about ten thousand a year. He was earning sixteen thousand a year when he quit, and he'd have gotten at least twenty-five thousand a year as manager of this research plant they're building."

"Still, Doug is developing his own business, Eve. That's important. You ought to know that being your own boss counts for something, too."

"Still . . ."

"I'm unable to advise you. Oh, I'd like to tell you to send him to Mr. Hill. And I'd like to see Mr. Hill send him back north. Listen, I've always been interested in you, you know that. But—"

Her eyes silenced him.

"Big brother Ken," he said, after a couple of minutes. "Well, all right, if that's the best I can do. I won't pretend to like it or even understand it, but I won't be unpleasant about it, either. Advice? All right. For what it's worth, send him to Hill with the deed and let events take their course."

Eve took part of the advice. She did send Doug Chalmers to Mr. Hill with the deed, but she went along nervously, too, to defend her own interests against the great man.

Jared Hill received them in his living room on a blustery October day. A good fire crackled on the hearth, shooting sparks up the chimney, sending an aromatic warmth into the great, paneled room. Mr. Hill waved them to comfortable chairs before the fire, quite poised, and quite handsome, too, if the coldness were ever to leave his gray eyes. "The nicest time of the year," he said affably. "Gather the harvest, enjoy the autumn colors, toast yourself before good oak fires. I've decided to remain here permanently, Eve. The research plant will be a nice amusement. So, in a sense, the five acres will be used for recreational purposes after all."

"So much fuss over so little," she rebuked him. "I'm not as proud as I used to be, sir, to know you. I think you could have behaved somewhat better."

"My crime?"

"You corrupted Supervisor Wilcox, sir. You left your daughter hanging, sir. You tried to cheat me, sir."

"No. To begin with, Supervisor Wilcox approached me only after he had begun the maneuver to possess your land. He corrupted me, not I him. As for my daughter. In what way was she left hanging? Her involvement in the matter was voluntary. She perceived, or thought she perceived, a chance to defeat you in an area where she imagined she had the advantages. What precisely could I have done to help her? The greatest corporation lawyer I've ever met said the thing was hopeless. The man brought down specifically to aid her, at my expense, mind, also told her the situation was hopeless. And, finally, it was my money, specifically, that enabled her to win a victory of sorts. I told her to pay fifteen thousand an acre; she got the land for twelve per acre."

Eve gulped.

"I'm rather fond of my daughter," Mr. Hill said embarrassedly. "And at the moment, if I may say it, I'm proud of her. She did snatch some small measure of victory from a hopeless situation, and no one can do better than that. Now she goes to Paris. The first of the year, she enters the company. I think that will please her. This competitive spirit of hers . . . well, hardly the spirit of a person made soft by luxury, eh?"

Doug Chalmers handed him the deed. Mr. Hill looked it over, looked him over more carefully. "Well, Doug," he said, "it ended a bit differently from the way we expected, eh? So it goes. One of the reasons business is so exciting to those hardnosed enough to welcome a good brawl. You never know for certain how a thing will come out. You hope you'll win, you think you'll win, but unexpected factors come into the thing and it all becomes fluid. What are your plans?"

"I thought I'd develop this agency first."

Mr. Hill pursed his lips. "I don't think there's much in that. Of course, it could grow. But such enterprises take too much of your time. You don't make money through the actual performance of work, you know. You set a thing up, hire someone to do the actual work, and go on to set something else up. The stock in trade of a millionaire, young fellow, is ideas."

"I have other ideas."

Eve noticed that Doug's eyes were guarded, that his smile wasn't quite genuine.

"What ideas, Doug?"

"Oh, you'll learn about them as they develop, sir. One thing I learned in your company is never to divulge a good idea to anyone."

"Ah, but I'm in semi-retirement now."

"I doubt it, sir."

"Dr. Hale and Dr. Hawkins will tell you so."

"Will they, now?"

Mr. Hill smiled appreciatively, but not with his eyes, never with his eyes.

Doug glanced at his watch. "That appointment won't wait," he told Eve.

Eve almost asked what appointment. But she checked the impulse and started to rise.

"Care to be general manager of my plant, Doug?"

Eve almost stopped breathing.

"No, sir."

Eve began to breathe normally again.

"Why not, Doug?"

"I've had it, sir."

"Aren't you rather young to say that?"

"Perhaps. Still, you have to stop sometime, don't you? Do you know what, sir? I was on the verge of asking Lois to marry me. How low can you get?"

"Lower."

"How much lower?"

"Had you married her, Doug, I'd have fired you and cut her off without a penny. Now get something straight. You're not the first two-bit fellow Lois took an interest in, and you're not the first fellow who planned as you planned. And I have news for you. I'm the fellow who lost a wife because of dedication to business. I'd hardly let my own daughter in for that, now would I?"

Doug smiled faintly. "I rather think not, sir. At any rate, it's all academic now, isn't it?"

"Why are you playing hard to get, Doug?"

"Am I?"

Abruptly, Mr. Hill laughed. Then he turned to Eve. "Do forgive me, young lady," he said. "Apparently the decision is yours to make. Take a look at the boy; he's drooling for that job. But will you approve?"

"No, sir."

"Think, now, think!"

Eve studied Doug's face. Disappointment there? How difficult to tell when you didn't know the man as well as you ought!

"I think you're playing with him, Mr. Hill," she said quietly. "You want him to accept. Then, after he's accepted, you'll laugh in his face. Of such spite, it would seem, are once great men made."

He ordered: "Get out of here!"

Eve rose with alacrity.

He apologized, of course. "Hang it," he said in a strange voice, "I'm alone and I'm lonely. It didn't please me to see Lois leave. She had to leave, of course. She was in love with you, Doug, or thought she was. But what have I, where am I? I don't like any of this at all."

"I'd want a five-year non-revocable contract, sir."

"My word is my bond."

Hurt, Eve thought: well, there it was. How odd it was that her dream, like Ken's dream, would remain but a dream!

She went quickly to the door. She slipped into her coat out on the big porch. As she stepped down to the blue gravel drive, it began to rain, and she remembered that way back in the spring, when all this had begun, she'd had to walk to work because Rod had been too angry to drive her as usual.

The next thing she knew, Doug was taking her arm quite cheerfully and steering her toward his Cadillac. "Never tell me in our old age," he said, "that you secretly wanted to be a rich woman. You had two chances to nod yes back there."

Eve smiled tremulously.

Doug drove her home by way of the river.